I0712830

BOOKS & SMITH
New York Editors

THE AMERICAN MYTH

EDGAR SMITH

A NOVEL

A Books&Smith Publication.

The American Myth

This is a work of fiction. All names, characters, places, and incidents are the product of the author's imagination and are used fictitiously. Any resemblance to actual people, living or dead, or to places or events, is entirely coincidental.

Distribution of this work, partial or in full, for any purpose and by any possible means, physical, electronic, virtual or otherwise, without the express written consent of the author is prohibited.

2023 © Edgar Smith
First edition 2023 Hardcover
All rights reserved by the author.

2024 © Edgar Smith
Second edition 2024 Paperback

Published by Books&Smith in the USA in 2024.
Cover design and editing: Books&Smith.

ISBN: 979-8-9889495-2-7

For Swamny.

Other books by the author:

Algunas tiernas imprecisiones (Poesía, 2013)

El palabrador (Cuento, 2013)

Island boy (Poesía, 2014)

La inmortalidad del cangrejo (Novela, 2015)

Versenal (Poesía, 2016)

Randomly, a poem (Poetry, 2016)

Cuentos raros (Cuento, 2016)

The Wordsmith (Short fiction, 2017)

Gnuj & Alt (Novel, 2017)

arrimao (Novela, 2017)

Verso y lágrima (Poesía, 2018)

Tandava (Poesía, 2018)

Puro Cuento (Cuento, 2019)

Voz Propia / Voice of our own (Poesía/Poetry, 2019)

La noventa (2020)

Por esta curiosa ventana (Cuento, 2021)

Through this strange window (Short fiction, 2022)

www.booksandsmith.com

What I am remembering, of course, is simple nostalgia, the universal desire to preserve, unbroken, those links that keep us connected to home and family, the first community we encounter, with its smells and flavors, its flora and the music of its daily life. But if it were no more than nostalgia, it would constitute a negative force, a vain attempt to stop time, enclose oneself in the past, and live in one's imagination, in an invented space where nothing changes.

No, the immigrant multiplies in another sense, or rather, in two others: outward, moving toward the new and unknown in order to master it, and simultaneously inward, in order to learn how to judge, but with new eyes, that lost past that nevertheless continues to exert its influence over his life and his thought.

Rhina P. Espaillat
from her Exordium of
poet Juan Matos's **The Man Who Left**.

IN RETROSPECT

While I was in my early teens, my grandfather never lost a chance to remind me of the importance of "being professional." This was what he called it: "being professional." And by that, what he strictly meant was that any boy or girl who intended to do good by their life ought to become either a doctor, a lawyer, an architect or an engineer. Nothing else would do. In his mind, which was a mind of his time, these were the only respectable careers—the only college careers that made sense and could bring status and, possibly, wealth. The latter, of course, was secondary. Being professional, see, that was the one thing that mattered.

I, too, had a mind of that time—which means that I was a teenager of that time –unable to see beyond my own nose–; and, being that the case, necessarily, I disagreed with my good old grandfather. Being a doctor or a lawyer was his aspiration for me. *His* dream. (It was his way of guaranteeing that we: my mom, my sister, and I, would have a future.)

I wanted none of that. I wanted to be a publicist. I wanted to make advertisements. I wanted to create and draw and come up with concepts and designs and then draw some more. I loved "the taste" of words as I pronounced them. I liked the shape and size of fonts, the amalgam of colors (the seemingly vast amount of shades and hues that derived from a single drop of blue or red), the harmony of elements when blended together into, say, a poster… I was in awe of catch phrases and mottos. I wanted to be like the models and the actors and whoever conceived how they should pose, stand, sit, crouch… I wanted to be rich and famous, and hang out with the men and women who spent their nights in hotels like the Sheraton or the Decameron.

But, you see, even in my wildest dreams, I still agreed with my grandfather on the core idea of it all: I wanted to be a professional. I wanted to go to college and graduate. I wanted to be addressed by whatever title the degree I would get could grant me.

However, just like my grandpa, I lacked vision. He was short-sighted because he never had a chance to reach higher education and thus be able to discern that any career I undertook would be good enough as long as I loved it and were passionate about it. I was short-sighted because I was still too young to understand his fears and frustrations.

As time went on, as the months and even years started to bump onto each other, overlap, and eventually accumulate like dust in the corners of our lives, as we realized that my dreams of "being professional" all but vaporized, my grandfather shifted his attention to my sister. I was always his boy, his good boy, but I was no longer the champion of his dreams. I had entered my twenties, and the closest I had managed to be around books was at my full-time job in a printing business. I had wasted my chances and he knew it.

I knew it, too. Even when, some mornings, I would wake up with a sense of rebellious determination and swore on everything sacred that I would re-north. I ended up standing at the threshold that led to the street, hands inside my pockets, looking at the all-too-common passage of existence, my eyes skimming over the details of La Baltasara Street—which I could never forget even if I tried.

Just like it did through me, Fate also made fun of my grandfather through my sister. The poor thing had been an even more ambitious wild horse than I. She wanted it all: the doctorates, the specialties, the wealth, the prestige… it lasted even less. It took but a semester for her to fall in love with some no-good dude, get pregnant, and lose the baby. And that was that. No career, no love, no baby, no future.

All she got out of it was a severe depression and an even more severe sense of loss and futility. Poor sis never understood that the game of life is not about winning but about playing as hard as you can just to get ahead for as long as you can. There is no winning. In the game of life, we play for brevity and for a fleeting sense of joy and fulfillment. Heck, one could say we play because there is no alternative: it is either we play as hard as we can or we do not even get to enjoy whatever allocated time life may have in store for us. Happiness is the word we made up to delude ourselves that there is a final goal. But whoever has been around long enough will tell you happiness is not a place where you will ever land or conquer. Happiness is a series of instances that you will encounter as you trek your way because, well, it's all about the journey, not the destination. Because there is no other destination than a coffin. Death is the only end and the only constant contender we face in the game of existing. And, sadly, the game is rigged. Death always wins in the end. I mean, Death is so sure it will win, it gives us a whole life in advance, doesn't it?[1]

After my sister and I failed to please my grandfather — and becoming professionals wound up being a chimera— it was Mariel's turn, my daughter.

---

[1] Translated from a verse in Spanish by Cancerbero—famous Venezuelan rapper.

Now the irony was that my grandfather was so old and disappointed that he no longer believed he would live to see his dream come true: nobody in his family had ever graduated from college. Nobody ever would, he thought, defeated. He himself had only completed five or six years of elementary school with the sole solace of having learned how to read and write. Nobody else before me had even come close to graduating from high school.

You may wonder, why was this so important to him? Well, it has to do with pride—perhaps even with a subconscious alertness regarding the severance of the circle of underperformance that ran deep in our family's history. All I know is that he was part of a group of men who had been friends for decades and who happened to be, every single one of them, lawyers or doctors. They all traveled the world together. They were inseparable. And even though they never made my grandpa's lack of education a thing, in the back of his head, it always was. Generally, even in their efforts (or lack thereof, which is the natural way of making someone feel they belong) to make him feel welcome, he often felt a tinge of condescension.

Was there ever such a thing? Who knows? Was it real for my grandpa? Sure, it was. Not because they acted like they were superior, but because in my grandpa's head, deep down, he felt that they were. He saw 'being professional' as the condition of higher men. And then there was the honor and safety that a professional diploma inexorably bestowed upon people. Being professional meant you would never go hungry. You would always be respected.

Mariel understood this concept, too. She was from a different breed, had real ambition. She was a smart, assertive, and beautiful young woman with aspirations neither my grandpa or I would ever comprehend. She wanted more from life than any of us could ever dream life owed us. For Mariel knew a key detail: life owed her nothing and offered her everything. She knew she was in a unique position to reach that other level and thus break the cycle: the cycle of poverty and undereducation that had plagued my family through generations. To be fair, this plague not only affected my family, it was present in most of the families of the underprivileged.

Well, Mariel knew all of this. She understood she was the very last bastion of hope for our legacy. She embraced the challenge. She shone. She sparkled and, in the process, ignited everyone else's hopes: maybe this time around, grandpa would get to see the long-awaited diploma.

And he did. Mariel graduated Suma Cum Laude, top of her class. Top of the entire college, probably. Grandpa was barely a year away from his eventual passing and well into his eighties. Whether he grasped Mariel's achievement in its entirety, we will never know. But he smiled like he understood what was happening. He held the diploma in one hand, a toothless grin on his eight-decade-old face, and hugged her and posed for the photos—his other arm, frail and wrinkled, around her, his head held high.

She wore a blue toga. The overdone make-up on her face made her look older. *Idiots, covering her natural beauty!* She smiled her lighthouse smile and lit up the whole room. As she walked along the other young men and women in a row that snaked around two aisles, the flashes of dozens of cameras went on and off at the same time, non-stop. The hall held hundreds. They sat with their hands on their laps, all dressed up—a collective veil of pride covering their grinning faces. Their postures, though uncomfortable, denoted how perfect the culmination of their years-long dream was turning out to be.

A month or so before graduation day, Mariel asked me the rhetorical question I had feared all along, "Pa, you won't make it to my graduation, will you?"

That night, my tiny rented room felt like it had crammed down to the point of suffocation.

And then came the night of the celebration. Who could have guessed the vastness of my sorrow? Could God himself guess the size of my impotence and frustration?

As I saw the pictures and clips on my tiny cell phone screen, my eyes became fountains. My head kept nodding and negating, randomly, unable to stay put. The knot in my throat felt like a dam—it was trying to contain a flood of screams from totaling the world around me. I was choking on my sadness. Dying of regret and shame and sheer anger.

No, I did not make it to my daughter's long-awaited, hard-fought graduation. More than twenty years before, I had decided to travel to New York in search of the American dream…

CHAPTER 1

THE BANK

"The worst? Christmas, New Year's Eve, all these damn days… The whole Holiday season is never easy," Ricardo said, his voice seemed to carry a slight echo in the width and silence of the resplendent white and gray Community Bank reception area.

Roberto, gun in hand, sat just a few feet from him. He looked exhausted. His broad shoulders slouched forth and his head, shaved off almost clean, hung close to his chest. A tiny puddle of blood had formed in the space between his legs and damped his pants. He had tight-wrapped a shred of his shirt around the wound. While Ricardo spoke, Roberto rubbed the crown of his head with his left hand. Eyes closed, eyelids heavy… he hadn't slept much these past three days.

"Of course, *primo*, as soon as you listen to any of these Christmas merengue songs, you feel some melancholy shit inside pulling at your heart. You know, Milly or El Mayimbe's merengue songs:

"cha chara chara, cha chara chara… Damn! *Esta navidad la quiero pasar contigo, amor, teniendo tu cariño, siento mi felicidad, esta navidad la quiero pasar contigo, amor…* man!

And there you are—thinking about everything and every single person you left behind," Roberto said. Something, he felt, took furious bites at his heart.

Ricardo would glance at Roberto every now and then. He did not know him, he was certain, but there was a familiarity to his face, some trait or gesture he could not specify yet made him wonder if maybe he had seen Roberto before. Or perhaps it was just an indescribable likeness that pertained to the average Dominican man, an aura if you will, that has nothing to do with skin color or certain facial shape, but had everything to do with attitude and poise. He realized, too, that Roberto had not thought this robbery through.

He tried to move his arms. They hurt. He felt dizzy. The two women were on the floor, three meters away. Fortunately, they had calmed down somewhat. Might have realized crying and whining was useless. From his spot, he could see the security guard's boots.

"It's the children one thinks about, isn't it?" Ricardo asked pensively—something dry crawling up his throat.

"I have a son, *primo*. It's been so damn long. Shit's so fucking hard. It's about to be Christmas and here I am, no money, no friends, no nothing. This is what it's come to," Roberto complained and sighed at the same time.

"It is never easy being away from one's children," Ricardo said somberly. He tried to say something else, but the knot in his throat kept getting bigger.

"Yeah, I know. Been four years away from my boy, ever since I came over. He was so tiny, my newborn. It's so fucked up, man! One comes over here thinking, you know, it's gonna be O fucking K, but, nah, it ain't. After all's said and done, this shit tests you."

The silence inside the bank battled against the noises from outside. Ricardo figured there was probably already a mob out there despite the cold.

'I know that things are different in these small towns—different from New York, I mean. Shit's not easy over there. In that damn city, everyone keeps to themselves. Everyone's like sleep-walking—in another damn world. Nobody cares if you fine, if you not. If you fall, they leave you right there, no one even tries to help. And I know, I know it's us. We mess things up by being petty and deceiving. People try to help but get their asses sued by the one motherfucker they giving a hand to. It's happened a million times.

It's the people, *primo,* I tell you. People cannot help but make our hearts turn to stone. Here's a little better. I would have come directly over here if I'd had the chance.

But, on the other hand, dude like me with no papers, what was I to get in a small town like this? Jail time is all. Because, you see, that's the other side of the coin: people are nicer here, yeah, but it don't mean they won't discriminate. They do.

The very first day I came, I was in this little *bodega* asking around for my cousin Monchi, may his soul rest in peace, and this redneck is looking at me like I'm about to steal something. Yo, seriously? That's why I flip and do crazy shit. You can't be *bueno, primo,* you just can't. Try to be a nice guy, they fuck you up.

Like, *primo,* I tried. God knows I tried. I came over with a plan, wanted to get that quick buck, ya feel me? But shit wasn't the same, so I straightened up and got me a nice job and all. But, again, it's the damn people, *esta jodía gente de mierda, primo,* they're all bad."

Roberto paused for a second. In his mind's eye he saw Shanikwa's irresistible smile, her ass hard as cold dry cement, her mocking words on the note: *see ya, luv*.

"Not only that, they're damn racists, too. They will deny it down to their death, but everyone's fucking racist here. And I mean everyone: whites, blacks, Asians, fucking Latinos. Lemme tell you, you walk into a *blanquito*'s place, they look at you funny. They ask you ten times how they can help you; and you, new to this shit, may think it's, you know, customer service. My ass! In white people's eyes, you brown or black, forget it, you're a thief and a thug.

Now, the hilarious part? Blacks are just as racist as the motherfucking *blanquitos*! Dirty asses think they're better than us, *Latinos*. Don't ask me why, man, no logic to it, they just do. It's like they feel they're entitled to some shit because their great great motherfucking great grandparents were slaves to some brainless white folks. Like, the fuck we got to do with that shit? We were slaves, too, bro! We were slaves before this country was even founded!

And then they act tough, gotta see'em, but only fight by jumping you, five to one, who ain't brave five to fucking one?"

Roberto remembered the taller kid's face. How innocent he had looked asking for directions to some sneaker store. And then that first punch on his left temple that made the entire world fade almost instantly. And then all four of them kicking him.

Ricardo kept glancing at him. Roberto's tone betrayed some old wounds. Ricardo knew the feeling well. He'd come to terms with all of it, the damn racism, the awful grip coming to this country manages on everyone when it comes to judging people. Sad shit.

He had loathed them, too: the *morenos*, blacks. He, too, had fallen prey to the claws of prejudice.

He sighed. It seemed like eons before. Like it all happened in a different lifetime—to someone else, even. But he knew the feeling well, despite the passing of time, it was still fresh in his memory. In his heart: how misguided he'd been, how easily the Media and the narratives out there manipulate those willing to listen. To listen and to accept. Like this guy.

"I walk past them, I'm always *chivo*, always *moca*, always on the lookout. One gets funny, I fuck him up, no questions asked. That's me, *primo, yo me doy y to la vaina*, and I'm fucking ready to die.

I'll tell you one thing, like it or not, racist or not, I'd rather get prejudiced by some white motherfuckers than jumped by a bunch of black kids."

Ricardo had heard it all before. Practically the same speech, verbatim. Almost all of his coworkers in *La marqueta*. Most of his acquaintances back in New York. They all disliked blacks. And he knew the animosity came from both sides. Had felt it many times, how he was stared at, how disdainful they were towards anyone who looked Latino. *Ignorance is worse than white privilege.*

And then he also thought about telling Roberto that he was wrong: generalization is wrong. Especially, when it comes to race, because no matter what you are: White, Black, Hispanic, Asian, whatever, there are bad people and good people everywhere. There are wise and ignorant people everywhere.

Ricardo knew, however, that this was not *La marqueta*. This was no social gathering where he could just interrupt and share his thoughts. This man, Roberto, well, this was no friend of his.

Roberto looked no older than twenty-five. He was shorter than Ricardo but much stronger. He looked his age in spite of his eyes: they were cursed with endless sadness—and, yet, they carried more anger than sorrow. He turned those burdened eyes toward one of the women, who had resumed her crying. He stared at her in silence, hands still on his head. His eyes went back to fixing on his boots and the puddle of blood. He was exhausted.

Ricardo kept glimpsing at the gun. Roberto seemed distracted, but with both of his hands tied, the older man knew he had no chance. Besides, he had not spent so many years in this country to come out now and play hero. No stupid kid would shoot him. He thought of his daughter and his mom. He was almost sure things would not escalate. Despite all of his crazy bravo talk, Roberto was surely an idiot, but he was no murderer. That thing with the security guard, it had been an accident.

"How long you been here, *primo*?" Roberto asked him, his voice dragging the burden of exhaustion.

"Twenty-four years."

Roberto whistled out of sheer surprise as the older man let out a sonorous, sad sigh. The woman kept whining like a scared little animal.

"June 28th, 1991. I had just turned twenty-six," Ricardo added, pensively.

"Twenty-four years is too fucking long, shit! I don't wanna spend so many years in this country, *primo*, with this damn cold cracking one's bones. *Es un bobo...*"

Despite the circumstances, Ricardo had to smile. He could not understand the expression Roberto had just used: *es un bobo*. It literally meant: 'it is a baby pacifier', which, of course, made no sense.

"I cannot understand you, young people, sometimes." Roberto's grimace evinced his pain. "When we say 'es un bobo', we're saying something is tough, complex," he explained.

"I see," Ricardo responded; and then asked, "What about you? When did you come?"

"Told you already, *viejo*, four years ago, 2010. My boy was fresh off the womb. If you see'im now, *coño*, time flies... *Primo*, how were things when you came? I remember there was this dude in my block, *en el patio*; he came over and, shit was wild, he said. Went back with everything. Dude hustled and got rich."

Ricardo tried to stretch his neck a little. He'd been in that same position for quite some time now and it sure felt uncomfortable. With his coat still on, he'd started to sweat.

"It was different, yeah. And what you say is true: that was the time of the infamous Dominicanyorks. Most of the men who came here back in the day came to hustle. Not everyone, sure, but most. And those who went back to *el patio* would fill our stupid heads with fantasies—we, who could only dream of traveling abroad—they told us there was money on the sidewalks, that there was a drug *punto* at every other corner and customers for everyone."

'Go figure," Roberto interrupted, 'Shit was all about selling drugs, getting rich or die trying way before 50 was game."

Ricardo, lost within his own monotone, did not even realize he had been interrupted. He finished by saying, "we back in the island believed every single word."

"What about you? You came here to hustle, too?" Roberto asked him, his eyes fixed on the shiny, drying blood.

"No, never had the balls. It was easier to get a visa back then—even a green card. My grandpa had a small business and knew a few people. Through him, I got a non-permanent visa. I had planned to spend a couple of months to check things out…"

Silence the size of a mountain fell between them suddenly. Ricardo broke it by saying, "longest fucking couple of months ever."

CHAPTER 2

DEFINITELY NOT NEW YORK

"Shut up, *coño*, you fucking deaf? You want me to blow your head off, is that it?" Roberto yelled at the brunette. He was by the windows. The wide, thick curtains prevented anyone from looking inside the bank. The police were out there. There was that intermittent circular motion of the red and blue lights. A few minutes before the lights, the insistence of their sirens, like a combination of lament and menace.

The brunette had resumed her wailing. The blonde slid her fingers through the brunette's hair trying to calm her down. The guard's boots were still in the same position. He had not moved.

Ricardo was nervous. He knew the brunette's crying did not help. All the opposite: it made Roberto even more desperate. He was already in the early stages of losing it. Every other minute, he turned toward her. The gun in his hand gripped in the most dangerous of ways: with fear.

Ricardo knew that, if things continued that way, it would all get out of control. His instincts told him he had to do something, say something, try perhaps to convince Roberto to let him talk to the crying woman. It was a matter of waiting for the right time.

"These fucking *monos*... *coño*!" Roberto said with a grunt. He felt like a small rat with a nervous breakdown. He moved from one end of the spotlessly clean room to the next, trying maybe to evaluate the situation. On his face—lit up every ten seconds by the lights from the police cars—it was evident he understood his circumstances. It was easy to imagine the scene outside: the bank surrounded by five or six police units and probably over a dozen uniformed men and women. The murmur coming from the street, in stark increment, belonged without a doubt to the various by-standers drawn together by curiosity. Curious, too, was the fact that they had yet to hear "a gringo's voice", as Ricardo called them, through a loudspeaker.

A sudden groan made everyone's head turn at the same time. It was the security guard. Ricardo exhaled with relief.

"Roberto, we need to get this man a doctor," he suggested.

"That stupid faggot! If he hadn't tried to be a superhero, none of us would be in this fucking mess! I would have just gone with my money and that's it! That racist asshole should just die!" Roberto complained.

"I understand, *mi hijo*, but in these circumstances, this man's death is the one thing you really do not want," Ricardo corrected.

Roberto continued to peek at the street through one of the corners of the curtains. Ricardo wanted to tell him that he should move away from the windows; that, if there were snipers on the rooftops, they would not hesitate to kill him.

He resisted the impulse. He did not know how Roberto would react. A cornered man is just like any other wild animal. Instead, he kept trying to save the security guard's life.

"I can check on him if you let me. See if I can stop the bleeding," Ricardo insisted. Roberto's mind appeared to be elsewhere. The gun in his hand swung back and forth with the impatience of a broken bell clapper.

From the corner of his eye, he glanced at the two women and then the street. The blonde had managed to quiet the brunette down one more time. Just the slight groans of the security guard were audible.

"Roberto," Ricardo pressed on, "this situation is already too dangerous, but if this man dies, it'll get much worse."

"That motherfucking faggot…" Roberto murmured.

He took a few steps away from the curtains and closer to Ricardo. His gaze hooked into the older man's eyes for a few seconds. Bending over with a knee on the floor and placing the gun down close to it, Roberto began to untie him.

As Roberto loosened the ties, Ricardo made the conscious effort of not looking at the gun. It crossed his mind, of course, as soon as he saw Roberto put it so close to him, to jump on him and try to seize it. He got rid of the idea right away: Roberto was physically much stronger. To tell the truth, Ricardo had never been one to brawl. This was no time to start.

Once the knot was undone, Roberto took back the gun. He pointed it at Ricardo, who disapproved with his eyes as he rubbed both wrists to stimulate his blood flow. Roberto gestured for him to go check on the security guard. Slowly, he got up and walked past the two women. The blonde one looked no older than thirty-five and the brunette was much younger. They all exchanged glances. There was a plea in the younger woman's eyes. She may have seen that, in Ricardo's eyes, there was nothing.

The security guard was bleeding badly. It was worse than Ricardo had assumed. The wound was close to the chest, luckily on the opposite side to the heart. Ricardo lost not one more minute. He took the shirt Roberto had teared up to cover his wound and did the same with the downed man, tightening it with all his strength. The poor man screamed in agony. The brunette immediately started to cry.

"Shut the fuck up, bitch! Shut up!" Roberto yelled. Everyone stole glances from one another. The blonde clenched her hand tight over the brunette's mouth. Roberto was already striding in their direction. Both women tried to retreat but their backs found the wall. Roberto grabbed the brunette by an arm and shook her repeatedly with great violence. He yelled in her face and scolded her the way one scolds a stubborn little child. In his other hand, the weapon swung madly as if awaiting orders.

"I swear on my dead mother I'll blow your head off, you cocksucker! Shut your fucking mouth!"

"This is Lieutenant Grant with the local police. You are surrounded. If you let the hostages go, we will take it as an act of goodwill and it will serve you well before a judge."

The gringo on the speakers. Roberto shook his head and let out a nervous chuckle. Ricardo looked at him. The expression of fear on Roberto's face was like some weird mask intent on staying put for good.

"Roberto, these people play no games, mijo, give up before…"

"Fuck all of them! And you, you don't give me no more advice, alright? Leave me the fuck alone!" Roberto yelled as he ran to the glass windows and cracked the curtain open just an inch.

The Lieutenant still held the loudspeaker. He was tall and lean, black, dressed in a suit not too visible under the navy coat. He was standing behind a black Chevy. Next to him, several police officers in their winter uniforms aimed their guns at the bank.

"Fucking monkeys!" Roberto mumbled, his shaking hand evinced the fear he was feeling. Ricardo, still bent over the security guard, kept thinking of a way to get this idiot to surrender. If he didn't, they'd kill him. An involuntary voice inside his head asked him why he cared what happened to the thief. No response came to mind.

"Roberto, listen to me. These people aren't playing. They don't care about your reasons, your race, or anything at all; not even us in here, trapped, they don't care. All that matters to them is resolving the situation in the fastest way possible. They only care about the illusion of efficiency and safety, to look good for the newspapers and the cameras. Let the people out there think they're safe, you know. If you don't surrender, we will all die."

"Shut up, old man, shut up already. If we gonna get fucked, so be it. These *maricones* won't pressure me. As long as ya'll here, they won't break in."

The security guard tried to move but the pain made him scream instead. Roberto yelled at him to shut the fuck up as he pointed the gun at him. The women, even more scared than before, resumed their sobbing. Roberto shifted his position. He looked around through the small opening between the thick curtains. Seemed indecisive on whether to attack or flee.

Lieutenant Grant spoke into the loudspeaker one more time. He was trying to convince him to give up. Roberto, in time, only managed to swing the gun, finger on the trigger, tremulous.

Ricardo signaled for the women to find cover behind a near pine desk.

Fear wouldn't let them move. They kept staring in Roberto's direction, kept looking at the hand with the weapon as it swung back and forth like some threatening pendulum: his finger almost pulling the trigger.

And then the noises coming from outside did not help to ease their nerves. They could hear people shouting words in the distance, which distance itself didn't allow them to decipher. And the lights, with their annoying spinning of red and blue, had started to make them dizzy.

The security guard woke up. He was in his early fifties, strong-built, with ripe banana-colored hair and freckles all over his face. He tried to speak, but Ricardo motioned for him to be quiet. Ricardo tried to gesture an explanation of the critical state of their situation, but the wounded man had no mind for it. Instead, he tried to speak again. He also tried to reach for his hip with his left hand.

"Stop," Ricardo whispered nervously, but the man had already started to groan. The two women would not stop sobbing either. All Ricardo could do was look at Roberto. Sweat running down his neck and temples like cold water.

Roberto whirl-winded away from the window. Everyone got startled. He pointed at the curtains and shot the gun twice.

The sound of glass shattering and spreading in all directions mingled with the sound of the gunshots, the screams of the women, and the cries of pain from the security man.

The crowd outside scurried about for shelter. Ricardo threw himself behind one of the marble columns as he shouted for the two women to go behind the desk. He wondered if the cops had gotten too close. He knew once Roberto started shooting, the police would follow suit. That right there had been his damnedest fear.

A few seconds passed. Hidden behind the column still, Ricardo could hear the motion of people outside. The Lieutenant's voice came on once more and Ricardo thought it sounded like Yahve's voice in the movies of The Bible stories. He was preaching for calm and sense. He asked for a cease-fire—even when his people hadn't shot a single round.

Ricardo was both shocked and relieved. *Definitely*, he thought, *this is not New York*.

CHAPTER 3

RICARDO: FED UP WITH THE ISLAND

When I heard Joaquín Balaguer had won the presidency of the Dominican Republic once again, my two hands sprung up to my head in a gesture of both despair and disbelief. With my eyes shut tight, I looked up, ready to yell and curse—as if trying to insult the entire planet.

I had already endured the government of President Jorge Blanco—later convicted for embezzlement, no less—as well as Balaguer's previous twelve-year period, with his humiliating charity games, his murders, and fake-ass naïve face, screwing the whole country up the ass.

Our only true hope had been Professor Juan Bosch. But Balaguer was an evil genius. I still remember the dirty, fabricated campaigns he orchestrated against Bosch. One in particular: a video clip, edited in such a way that, when the professor was asked if he believed in God, his answer was doctored to be, *no, I don't believe in God.* It was repeated every fifteen to twenty minutes in every major television channel Balaguer could buy off. It played constantly until ballot day.

Balaguer's ingenuity was based mainly on a fascinatingly deep understanding of the Dominican people's idiosyncrasy and psychology. In a country with a vastly catholic population, this simple trick cost the good old professor hundreds of thousands of votes.

Of course, to ensure victory, the old blind wizard also hired a full team of Resuscitators—people in charge of miraculously making the dead cast their votes. He hired magicians to clone IDs and mathematicians to alter quantities in the results. There was simply no possible way for poor and decent professor Bosch to win.

Yet, we had hopes. The situation was so chaotic that it took very little for us to find hope. I recall that, at the moment of entering my vote in the urn, I experienced a flashback: it was the April strike once again, back in 1984. I was transported to Villa Juana, to aunt Margot's house. I was nineteen again in my mind's eye. Saw the policemen in gray uniforms shooting at the protestants. Three of them behind a building. One had a shotgun. The other two, revolvers. They took turns shooting but didn't even dare or care to look at whom they were trying to kill. Never asked themselves why either. Why they were shooting at the people—the poor people just like them, protesting for things that would benefit them and their families as well.

I remember my aunt pressed me against her bosom. Told me not to speak, covering my mouth with one hand. By then, the news of the strike had spread everywhere. A shortwave radio that belonged to my cousin Joselo (paraplegic in a wheelchair) captured every now and then the news provided by Radio Mil or Radio Popular—two of the only three or four radio stations in the whole country—about the incidents and confrontations taking place in towns such as Sánchez Ramírez, Moca, La Vega, Valverde Mao, and Salcedo…

That night, we all slept together in the same room, on the floor, a single mattress on top of us, as if bullets could not go through it and kill us anyway.

We had to pour water on our faces to breathe due to the smoke from the burnt tires the strikers used as protest and the tear-gas bombs the police threw as retaliation. Any strange noise or gunshot woke us up and kept us on edge.

On the morning of April 25th, the last day of the strike (of *La Poblada, The Town Gathering,* as Professor Bosch had named it), cousin Joselo died. He was found sternly still, wet in his own urine, detached from the grips of life.

Although he died of cardiac arrest, I never got over the sensation that the strike had killed him.

That afternoon, a hoarse-speaking anchor from Radio Popular announced it was all over. The count of casualties surpassed the hundred.

Later that afternoon, I arrived home. My grandpa, even before hugging me and giving in to weeping, slapped me. It was a sign of frustration, impotence, fear, and love. It was the only time he ever laid a hand on me. Three days before, without permission, I'd stepped out of the house and on to my *tía*'s. The poor old man had had no idea where I was, whether I was dead or alive.

I recalled all of it on that 16th of May, at the exact moment of casting my vote. The next day, when they announced Balaguer the winner, I told myself I had to get away from the Dominican Republic.

CHAPTER 4

BRAINWASHED

To fully understand the crisis that pushed us out and away from the homeland, it seems necessary to recount a little bit of history: in 1844, with the Dominican independence from Haiti, the Dominican peso was introduced. Up until then, the Haitian gourde had been used as the official Dominican currency. The peso was decimalized in 1877.

In 1891, Ulises Heureaux, A.K.A. Lilís, then president of the Dominican Republic, introduced the franc. It was probably a strategy, a diversion: the man had been embezzling for a while.

The franc never substituted the peso —as the American dollar later did, specifically in 1905. Each dollar was worth five Dominican pesos.

Another version of the Dominican peso was later introduced, the peso oro, which brought along all current bill denominations, from $1 to $2,000.

At the beginning, the value of the peso oro concerning the American dollar was practically the same. However, in a lapse of twenty years, from 1984 to 2004, approximately, the peso oro went from $1.45 to $37.50 per dollar.

So, the economic crisis, including the festering of livelyhood, the rise of housing, and the cost of prime food were the principal reasons for migration. I remember reading that it had all started as early as the sixties.

In the 80s, it became so easy to enter Europe that the USA migration focus was slightly derailed. However, the 90s were all about *the fever* of the United States exodus. This, of course, included illegal travelers.

Everyone had started to visualize a quickly-darkening future in the homeland. Balaguer's constant presence in power (fueled by fraud), violence by the police, the recurrence of protests, manifestations, and strikes, and the unbearable rise of food costs, among many other things, channeled the fantasies of finding a better life abroad.

Add to those things what has been labeled as 'The Americanization' (the consumption of American art, name-brands, music, films, fashion…) of our national culture, which began in the 80s or earlier; and the return home of the *bregadores* or *Dominicanyorks*, who came back to the island with their *cordones* (really thick gold chains), their shiny shoes and their many, many dollars, which, upon exchange, turned out to be fortunes. Those were the ones who really poisoned our minds. We would do anything to become these dudes. Many of us would do anything to get the money for a *machete*, even a trip in a *yola*.

****

In January of '91, on a breezy Saturday, a man wearing a shirt of a fabric we used to refer to as *Charlie* (a name no one ever bothered to confirm) and *mahones* or *mahomas* —these were the names my mom used back then for denim—showed up in our 'hood. He had two-color moccasins and his hairdo was what people called a *Sasun*, a name probably Dominicanized from Sassoon or some such. The truth was this dude's hair had more gel and Brylcreem than John Travolta's full array of characters blended all together.

The shirt, which seemed to dance easily at the slightest movement of his body, was unbuttoned down to his abdomen. On his chest, sliding down from his shirt collar ("coincidentally" upturned) gleamed a 24K, obese, gold chain.

Now this dude was thin and tall, and walked with a premeditated limp, which we all agreed looked ridiculous, but ended up imitating anyways.

As he walked, he called the names of most of the old folks from our street: Sandra, Margó, Meri, Maricrí, Leonidas… and those he called, he went and hugged. He smiled at them and engaged in conversation for minutes that knew no end. He looked like a truly kind-hearted fellow at that moment. Shared embraces, kisses, pats on backs, and some serious laughter. Slowly, everyone got out of the alleyways and patios, and in no time, our friend found himself surrounded by the good old people of La Baltasara Street. Just like a celebrity would.

I was with two of my friends. We were playing checkers outside my house. Abu, my grandpa, on his rocking chair, told us our visitor was Nelson's son, the youngest, who'd gone to New

York a few years back with a machete. Abu said his nickname was *El Corbejú*.

When the guy saw me, he came up to me and, with more strength than I'd thought him capable of, hugged me and lifted me off the floor, as his laughter and efforts to get my name right filled the ears of everyone in a square mile. It took me half an hour and many an anecdote to finally remember who he was. Dude looked totally different.

El Corbejú was barely two or three years older than me. Although he remembered me with apparent affection (I could not comprehend why), my recollections of him were limited to his label as a "presence", a "figure" of the neighborhood, like El Rulli perhaps or the infamous Santico: hoodlums who'd done so much mischief and caused so much trouble they had become urban legends.

Perhaps, I philosophized, there was no real affection, but that was his idea of vindication with the neighborhood, with his history within it. As if by getting close to me, one of the "serious ones", somehow, he'd manage to erase the things he'd done, who he had been, and what he represented. Maybe the fact of being back with money, whatever the means he got it: selling drugs, killing people even, made him think he could aspire to some sort of redemption. I did not understand what kind of redemption he could expect from me: I had nothing to give or take, but I guess this is how we are: once we extend an olive branch, we instantly expect peace. As if a little branch could remove the past.

He asked me if I wanted a cold one (as he drew from his pocket an obscene amount of fifties and hundreds), and told one of the beer-lickers hovering around like albatross to go fetch a few Presidentes. I made a timid motion with my head that meant

Why not?—when you don't want to be seen as a beer-licker yourself. My grandpa gave me the evil eye in frank disagreement.

El Corbejú laughed that afternoon at every silly thing we said, bought beers for everyone, and handed out a couple of thousand pesos among the old and the leeches.

Before he left, as Willie Colón's *Che Che Colé* played in the background, I asked him about New York.

With the same nonchalance he used for everything else, he said that The Big Apple was *the world.*

"One should not die before seeing New York," he said with the airs of a bohemian philosopher, "he who does dies blind."

*****

The encounter with El Corbejú motivated me in a highly unexpected way. Without a second thought, I set out to research about the *yola* trips and the infamous machetes.

In a matter of days, these options had been discarded. The risks were simply too high.

My curiosity nonetheless kept me going full throttle, pushed me to collect stories from other people in the neighborhood who had tried to leave the country one way or the other. As I dug on, the yarns multiplied (this is when my first suspicions surged that many of these guys could have become accomplished writers) and grew in complexity and boldness. Surprisingly, one of those stories, the one I thought most incredible, turned out to be true:

Alá, a friend of ours, recounted the whole thing (may God keep him by his right side, resting from this ingrate world), one of those nights we got together to play dominoes. He said the guy's name was Rafael and his future had not been a promising one. The police had taken him in a couple of times over street fights and petty thefts. He had a brother from his father's side, Julián, whose mother turned out to be *gringa*. Julián had been living in New York for many years. Alá said that Rafael and Julián were two identical drops of water: that's how much alike they looked. It did not matter that one was three years older. It took a really good eye to tell one from the other.

When Rafael was sent his brother's passport, no one could categorically deny that this wasn't his photo on it.

As Alá told the story, my mind visualized it. It is a habit that I have to get ahead (in my head) of the story being told. I asked myself, for instance, if an expert in documentation would not be able to discern that said photography belonged to a different person. I wondered if the training of the immigration officials could be so easily breached. Surely, I told myself, situations of this nature have been considered at the moment of establishing security measures.

Alá arrived then at the crucial moment of the story. He said that Rafael and Mildred—his sister, who had lived in New York her whole life and brought him the passport—arrived at the airport together. They spent twenty minutes in line and finally met with an immigration officer, who immediately scrutinized both the passport and Rafael's face. After a few expected questions that the officer directed at Mildred, he stamped a departure seal on one of the back pages and wished them a safe trip and a full recovery. Upon arrival to the United States, the scene unfold-ded almost identically.

Despite my silent questionings, it never crossed my mind that, once in New York, Rafael would have to face the American immigration officers or that he would be interviewed in English (since Julián's was an American passport). But some people's cunning is just ridiculous. Rafael did not have to answer a single question. He could not. He had traveled under the guise of a di-sabled person: bound to a wheelchair, his head wrapped in gauze. He appeared to have had an accident: his jaw crossed by thin iron rods that held it together. Clearly, he couldn't talk. He looked like a yet-unfinished mask of Pinhead.

It was Mildred who showed the officials the documents that validated her brother's condition and identity. It was she, al-so, who answered all their questions.

*****

One afternoon by mid-February, I was perusing over a Popular Mechanic magazine (waiting to be told where to place some brake wires I awkwardly held in my left hand) when my grandfather asked me why I was so interested in traveling to New York. He had probably overheard one of the dynamic conversa-tions I used to sustain with my friends.

"Pero, Abu, this country is doomed. It's got nowhere to go," I answered without urgency or conviction.

41

We were in the backroom, what we used to call *el cuarto de los ratones* (The mice room), which my grandpa used as storage. We were in the process of putting away some wires—Abu's business was to sell spare parts for Lambretta and Vespa motorcycles—, when I heard him say, "You are right about that. These crooked politicians won't do nothing for us. But New York is no paradise, either. You've heard the stories."

I replied, "True, but they come with money, Abu."

He looked at me kind of sadly and said, "Only God knows how they get all that money, *mi hijo*. I want nothing to do with dirty money. I'd rather be poor my whole life. And I expect you to think the same way."

Abu was a man of clear convictions. He'd been born and raised in a small, poor town. By fifteen, when his dad left their house for good, chasing after some young ass, my great-grandmother brought him to la capital, to live with an aunt. He finished 6th grade and that was it, that was the extent of his whole education. Poverty did not allow for more. He had to go out on the streets to clean shoes and sell newspapers to help put food on the table. As an old man now, he's always said that those years taught him about honesty and hard work.

'Now, if you really want to leave, I'll help you. I'll talk to Homero. He knows about those things. Let's see what can be done."

I raised my eyes slowly, half-expecting him to be joking. I then stared at him incredulously, "Abu, you said Homero? The lawyer?"

He nodded as if suggesting that this man's help was just the natural thing to do. "Yes, mi hijo, Homero has been working for years with the people at the US embassy. He might be able to help."

The conviction in his voice, however naïve, was enchanting.

I knew this Homero character. A buffoon of a lawyer who spent his days betting on horse races, on baseball and basketball games, and on absolutely anything a man could place a bet on. Abu said that Homero, if given the chance, would bet on a winking contest.

The little hope I'd had when I heard him speak of help vanished at the mention of said clown. But Abu would not have it. He said one thing had nothing to do with the other. Abu vouched for Homero as a lawyer. I did not believe a word of it, but it was best not to argue.

Abu's business occupied a small room on the left side of the house. He did have his customers: loyal and grumpy old men who argued loudly over prices and baseball, and whose motorcycles were as precious to them as their own children. Time, of course, sides with decay, and technology helps with the substitution of things and people. The new brands of bikes, much faster than poor Abu could ever suspect, swallowed the older, slower competition. Add to this the fact that the old man refused to adjust to the changes. He rebelled against the newcomers and rendered, thus, himself and his business obsolete.

I wondered more than once (as I grew up), how he had managed to give my mom, my sister, and me (we were all born in that house), the quality of life we enjoyed. That business seemed to me so little, so tacky, and yet, it pushed us forth, paid for our private schools and our nice clothes, and never failed to put three meals on our table.

But, because of the things listed before, it eventually shut down and poor old Abu no longer had any money to give us. That's when I had to drop out of college and get myself a job at a small press. It was a job for dogs, with a miserable salary, but, at least, it paid enough to help with the food. Abu was then almost seventy years old or close. "Any day now," my mom would say now and then, "he'll go." When I thought about that, about every little sacrifice he made for us, that's when the hunger of going away from that shithole of a country assaulted me most fiercely.

New York. The damn Dominicanyorks had brainwashed me with their gold chains and their bullshit.

CHAPTER 5

ROBERTO'S TURNING POINT

Roberto was fifteen when his father stabbed his mother nine times. She had been cheating on him with some dude people called *Chulo*, a clerk at the local grocery store, *el colmado de Felo*.

Marcia survived. Augusto spent four long years in *La Victoria*—the most infamous and crowded prison in the country. The morning he got out, he went straight to Marcia's backyard and macheted her dead.

Those who saw the body said her head hung from the neck by a fine thread of flesh, in the most awkward of angles.

Roberto was in high school when it happened. He was repeating his last year for a second and final time. By the time he arrived home, they'd already taken her for the autopsy. He saw her in the morgue. Hours later. Her countenance resembled a caricature of she who, in life, had been his mother. She had make-up on (never before had he seen her wearing make-up) and someone had chosen the appropriate white blouse—it covered the sutures required to reposition her head.

She had, Roberto noticed, a vacuous expression. The unmoved countenance of someone going through something they found themselves entirely indifferent to.

He wept. He wept until he had no strength left. His sadness was, however, modest in comparison to his hatred.

The police found Augusto two days later. He had been hiding in the *conucos*. They sentenced him to life in prison without parole. That night, Roberto sat down and cried with no restraints. He'd sworn by his mother's lifeless body to avenge her death.

Roberto dropped out of school and jumped right into the street. In no time, he was hanging out with the *tígueres* by the corner. Those closer to him tried to advise him, tried to make him see this wasn't the life his mother would have wanted for him. But Roberto would not listen. From the moment of his mother's death, he never again listened. The only voice he could hear, a suffused voice inside him, told him there was but a single path toward the attenuation of his pain: killing Augusto.

There was, in his head, a twisted kind of logic: if he managed to make enough money, he would be able to either have Augusto killed in prison or buy his freedom to murder him himself. Nothing more occupied his mind.

It did not take long for him to own his first drug spot. And then another one. And another… in barely three years, his fame as a ruthless capo had peeked. Word on the street was that he was a *sicario*, a merciless assassin. The truth is Roberto controlled most of the drug sold in the 'hood, however, his reign wasn't built on blood-shed, but guile. He knew the only way to gain respect out there was through the perception of fearlessness and cruelty. Only the true psychopaths got away with what he'd set himself to accomplish, and that involved giving others the impression that he was willing to do anything to become the number one motherfucker in the hood, the *capo di tuti capi*, Dominican version.

So, instead of spreading death, he spread rumors of his total lack of mercy or regret. He had to beat the shit out of some jackasses, yes, because the truth was he knew no fear and his thirst for vengeance was such —he knew in his heart that, if it came to that, he would shoot some motherfucker dead, no remorse—, but (if only they knew) he had never killed a single soul. So, the other dealers respected him. They were convinced that Roberto was a man to stay friends with.

It was in those days that he met Ruth. A month into their relationship, they moved in together. Ruth reminded him of his mother in some ways. She had sad deer eyes and a childish smile. She liked children and, like his mom, preferred soap operas over discotheques.

The same day Ruth told him she was pregnant, he got caught by the DNCD—the Dominican version of the DEA.

They found a kilo of cocaine in his car and locked him up for what would be a full preventive year until trial.

Yet in barely eight months, he got out. Ruth was huge then. They hugged outside the prison building and cried for five minutes. Roberto had paid a small fortune to one of the corrupt lieutenants to get him out—this was the way business was conducted at these levels.

Once back, he realized the neighborhood had changed. Those who feared or respected him before looked at him now with an open sense of mockery, even menace. Those who had followed him belonged now to new gangs. There was no room for him anymore and he knew word had leaked that he wasn't who he'd made everyone think he was. He knew he just couldn't bullshit his way into that world again.

As he waited in line to buy fried chicken from the local Chinese place one afternoon, he ran into his cousin Nilo. Now this Nilo dude was one of those guys everyone knows and likes, an influencer of real social life, a man of the people. They spoke for a while about the tragedy, prison, and how different it all was on the streets... Eventually, Nilo talked to him about making a trip to New York.

"I'm leaving in a couple of months. If you are like me, let's go. Get the money and we'll do it through Mexico."
"How much?" Roberto asked.
"$150, 000," Nilo said.
"What, bro, that's a lot of fucking money," Roberto replied.
"I know, but there's a lot more in New York."

The trip was delayed for several months until one sunny afternoon Nilo showed up to ask for Roberto's passport and the money. Roberto was hesitant at first, but Nilo's demeanor was always conciliatory and convincing. The man knew how to talk. Roberto gave him what his cousin requested and Nilo disappearred again for three more months.
Roberto tried to take it easy. He did fear that Nilo would just "elope" with his money but, in truth, there was nothing he could do other than hope his cousin would come back.

Since there was nothing in the streets for him, he got himself a job as a security guard at a club. It was easy money. He didn't do much and most guys knew him. They caused no trouble—other than the occasional joke about his past. Besides, contrary to the average street guy, he'd been smart enough to save some good money under his wife's maiden name—to prevent it from getting seized by the authorities.

Those were the most peaceful months of his life. His son, Daniel, was a healthy and handsome boy. He spent as much time with them as he could. His son had brought hope and a sense of responsibility previously unknown to him. Although he never stopped thinking about avenging his mother's murder, the conviction of it had withered. To his surprise, he found himself genuinely happy at times—and he could just not believe it. At some point, even the trip had started to seem like something he didn't need to do.

Yet, when Nilo came knocking on their door that fateful Thursday at 10:00 PM, Ruth knew right away her life would go tumbling down a cliff. Roberto barely thought about it. Nilo knew what to say, what buttons to touch. There are people like that, puppeteers, masters at pulling the fragile strings of our emotions. Roberto placed a soft kiss on her lips and, staring into his toddler's eyes, told him to behave and to take care of his mom.

Little Daniel looked at his dad with watery eyes, as if he understood this was a farewell.

CHAPTER 6

VISA PARA UN SUEÑO

Homero, the lawyer, was a midget. With favor and sacrifice from mother nature, the man was barely five feet tall. He was so thin that, soaking wet, he must have weighed a little over ninety pounds. He had an annoying Hitler-like mustache and combed whatever little hair he still had towards the left of his weirdly-shaped head. His was the voice of some unpublished Disney character—he spoke so fast that he barely breathed between sentences. Homero was wearing a suit when he arrived that afternoon, tie included, and, as expected in the Caribbean weather, was sweating copiously.

Abu had convinced me to hear Homero out. I, knowing I had nothing to lose, agreed to it. Yet his sole presence drove me off edge. The little man was one of those people who look at you over their shoulder as if in the presence of some disgusting bug.

He took a seat in one of the way-too-many-times-refurbished armchairs in the living room. The fan whirred and whirled at full speed. The Virgen Mary in the painting seemed to stare at us with curiosity or plain anger.

Homero brought along an envelope that, clearly, had seen better days. At that precise moment, the man was wiping the sweat off his forehead with a square-patterned handkerchief that, along with his Florsheim shoes, must have caused havoc in the fashion world of the previous century.

I had to endure long minutes of their discussions on horse track race, boxing, the socio-political situation, Doña Meri (the
old lady neighbor who despised young kids), and Negro Delia,
who was crazier by the day…

At some point, finally, they spoke about me and my desire of travelling abroad. The good lawyer, with a Czar's flair,
meditated about his response for long seconds before once more
changing the subject and asking if mom had at long last made
coffee. He then said that, being Abu such a close and dear friend,
it might be possible for him to reach out to his contacts in the
American Embassy and Consulate. This was followed by an
insufferable litany of, I guessed with great effort, his resume and
personal accomplishments in the world of laws and tribunals.

In the forty minutes he spent there, he did not say a
single concrete thing; so, I had to take his word that he'd find out
if something could be done for me to obtain that visa. As soon
as he finished his second cup of coffee, he stood up and, not even
glancing at me, offered Abu his farewells—not before making an
ill comment about the Lions: Abu's favorite baseball team. I
noticed that Abu tried to reply but apparently couldn't think of
anything worth saying.

*****

To my utter surprise, eight days later, this dude phoned to say I was to go to the Consulate in exactly nine days, on March 9th, at 11:00 a.m.

He said to bring my passport, four photos 2 x 2, and RD$5,000.00 pesos—which back then was short of a fortune.

Also, I was instructed to ask the security fellow at the gate for Mr. Wolf.

When Abu told me these things, my first reaction was incredulity. I thought the douche bag lawyer had perhaps noticed how I'd looked at him, how lowly I thought of him, and had decided to have me bribe a consul, so I'd be thrown in jail. I sucked at my teeth loud and Abu asked what the matter was. I just shrugged.

Twenty minutes later, on my bed, with a thread of sunlight intent on blinding me, I had already started to think about the whole thing. By then, of course, with a little bit of hope. *Coño, what if this clown is serious?*

From doubts, I jumped to daydreams. I lay on my bed facing up, the patterned sheet half-covering my chest, with a knee pointing upward and my right arm behind my head. My left arm was my shield against the sun, which braved itself into the room through too many thin crooks and crevices on the wooden walls.

In my daydream, I saw myself walking placidly through wide streets in a city that not in the slightest resembled the city of Santo Domingo. This new city was enormous, rich, clean… I pictured myself walking alongside a multitude of people, all Dominicans, whose style of walk and dress emulated those of El Corbejú; and we walked on the cleanest sidewalks anyone has

52

ever seen, by humongous buildings whose rooftops were impossible to spot. There were *friquitaqui* carts along the sidewalk, and people, all smiles and nice words, who sold *equimalitos* and fruits. Some cars rode by slowly, so that I could wave *hi* at the drivers and they all waved back with a nice grin. I think I saw some of the *tígueres* from the neighborhood: la Aguja, Negro Delia, el Chu, all hanging out by some corner, smoking Montecarlo and discussing Pedro Guerrero and his records; and other sports, too, and the bullshit of politicians everywhere. At some point, I bent down to pick up a twenty that came toward me hopping here and there in the wind—and I realized I couldn't even daydream this stupid money in dollars.

And thus, I surprised myself smiling foolishly for a long while—as one who's just gotten the best news of their life.

*****

On March 9th, at 8:46 a.m., I was standing outside the Dominican Consulate. I was wearing, as was the norm at the time, my Sunday's best. With me, I had brought a mustard-yellow envelope where I kept the requested money (surely all of my grandfather's savings), my passport, and the photos—of which I did not approve.

My knees were shaking. Barely twenty feet away, there was a line of at least a hundred people. All waiting to enter. I could not help but hear, in my mind, Juan Luis Guerra's voice singing *Visa para un sueño.*

Not quite understanding why (and despite my efforts of reading the paperback edition of José Ingeniero's *El hombre mediocre*, which I had brought along to separate myself from the herd), something found its way inside me that seemed to cruise through my chest, stomach, and throat. It was something in the nature of a bad omen, a sense of sorrow, apprehension or some such, which did not allow me to breathe in peace for the following twenty-five minutes, the amount of time I had to wait until, finally, the so-called Mr. Wolf showed up.

All along, the only other thing I could think of was Mariel, my little daughter. *I'm doing this for you, baby.*

Now Mr. Wolf was no shorter –it seemed to me, really– than fourteen feet. He was so thin that, in a contest of the thinnest man alive, they would have given him first place without even looking at the other participants. He greeted me amiably and told me, in the funniest version of Spanish ever, that I was early, which is extremely unusual for Dominicans in general—a stereotype hard to undo. He asked my name and requested the envelope. His eyes asked if everything was in it and I nodded. Without making sure, he smiled, winked, and strode toward the building.

The time I waited for Mr. Wolf, no less than a half-hour, I spent trying to guess the exact manner in which I would be taken out of that place and straight to jail. I rehearsed, so to say, the answers I would give when they asked me how in the devil's name I had conceived the idea of trying to bribe an American Consul. Needless to say, none of the answers that came to mind was remotely satisfactory.

Mr. Wolf strode back out of the building accompanied by an older lady of an Oriental countenance and upset expression. They seemed to be in the process of a discussion of some sort. I squeezed Ingeniero's book so hard that I thought the words would spill down to the ground and, forever, get lost. When they arrived at where I was, the woman looked at me with what I thought were accusing eyes.

Oh fuck! is all I thought.

But the Chinese lady —anyone with slightly Oriental traits is 'Chinese' to us— just kept going, not a word uttered; and Mr. Wolf paused for barely twenty seconds to give me back my passport.

With an amused grin on his face, in that funniest of Spanish dialects, he said, "eta china de miergda," ("This fucking Chinese chic!"), and laughed out loud.

And just like that, he turned around and took his leave. And I stood there contemplating the visa that would take me to the United States of America.

CHAPTER 7

FLASHBACK TO THE ROBBERY

Roberto stepped in the Community Bank at around five-fifty that evening. Outside, the wind reached eighteen degrees Fahrenheit and the sun had set fifteen minutes before—obedient to the routines of winter.

The bank was located on the first floor of a twelve-story building—one of the few really tall buildings in town. A smaller edifice, used as a sort of communal warehouse for the bank and several other businesses, connected to the first one from the back through various doors and stairs. Whoever realized the two structures were like Siamese siblings would have guessed they belonged to the same owner.

The brunette and the cashier (the blonde) had been lively talking while their transaction was being processed.

Ricardo waited in line, six feet away from the brunette, watching a silly video and some photos on his cell phone—he had not made up his mind about how much money he would send Mariel, his daughter. *She deserves a healthy sum. Better to start her new married life without money worries.*

The Security guard's eyes were fixed on the street. He was concerned about the temperatures dropping even lower.

His thoughts were interrupted when Roberto stood by his side and put the cold mouth of the gun to his neck—all the while shouting his intentions.

Ricardo slid his cell phone in his front pocket and instinctively glanced at the cashier who, against all rehearsed security training, raised both of her hands and forgot to push the hidden panic button.

Five minutes before, the bank manager, Mr. Ben Carson, tall, slender and of an aristocratic pose, who looked ten years younger than his sixty-four, had stepped out with a certain urgency to the nearest MD Care Unit —not even ten minutes away— due to intestinal discomfort.

When Ben returned, he immediately realized something was wrong: the door to the bank was locked from the inside and the curtains run, shutting the view in from the outside.

Mr. Carson didn't call the police right away. He wasted, instead, a few minutes trying to peek through the curtains, just like a restless child intent on seeing a specific toy on Christmas.

Only when Mr. Carson heard the shot did he run full throttle, grabbed his cell phone, and dialed 911.

After disarming the security guard and making sure that Ricardo was no threat, Roberto turned his attention to the cashier, who'd already been filling in a duffel bag with both brand new and wrinkled bills.

It took the guard but a minute to realize Roberto was a rookie (giving him his back like that, leaving his hands free.) He grabbed the knife he kept hidden in the holster strapped to his left boot.

Maybe the expression of horror on the cashier's face gave the attacker away.

Roberto turned around and the shock of seeing the man right upon him made him pull the trigger. The bullet flew into the man's wide chest, but he'd been coming with such force that he still trampled Roberto and both fell. The women screamed like crazy. Ricardo took a few steps back, conscious that Roberto still held the gun and could start shooting out of nervousness.

Even badly hurt, the guard thrust the knife with brute force. Roberto dodged it by an inch or two. Yet the guard's second attempt reached the thief's right thigh and plunged into it viciously.

Roberto howled in pain. Out of sheer instinct, he pointed the gun at his assailant's head. There seemed to be an instant close to the suspension of time. A parenthesis, if you will, in which time did not exist. In that momentous halt of existence, Mike Smith, the security guard, stared at the dark round mouth of the gun. When a thing like this takes place, when time stops, one might still be capable of thought. If that is indeed the case, then Mike thought about his own death or recalled perhaps some utterly important duty he'd ought to attend to yet the expeditiousness of life had pushed away from memory; maybe he even managed to think of his family or about, who knows, some neglected thing, a weirdly irrelevant and innocuous one…

But there was no shot.

Roberto hit him hard on the right temple with the butt of the weapon and Mike passed out. He then looked around at the rest of them and, his hand on the leg wound, stood up—as he yelled for them to move away from the windows.

CHAPTER 8

MEET THE CAPITAL OF THE WORLD

The thing I recalled most clearly of the summer evening I arrived in New York was the unbearable heat. I had never heard the expression 'Humidity level.' But barely twenty minutes in, my cousin Gustavo, who had gone to pick me up at the airport, had mentioned this "humidity" at least seven times. It felt like he was talking about some mysterious woman who'd come to hurt us.

The heat in New York felt even worse than that of Santo Domingo. I supposed it was thanks to the mysterious humidity, which felt like some dense and heavy thing in the air trying to suffocate me.

Gustavo, driving his Chevy Nova (sky blue, 1963), told me, during the forty-minute ride to his apartment, everything that in his judgment ought to be known about The "Great" Apple. In his incessant discourse (as I admired the uncanny mixture of derelict-looking buildings, in-process constructions, the impossible amount of private cars and taxi cabs, and, eventually, an impressive skyline from an even more impressive bridge), he did not omit family gossip, political affairs, jokes with intricate plots, legends of the city, amazing feats by Dominican baseball players, and even some odd details, such as the price of haircuts and the address to some woman named Karla, who read the Tarot and the palm.

When we finally arrived in the Bronx, night had already fallen. I thought for a second that it was strange not to feel anything. Being in New York did not feel any different than being in the island. I did not know what I'd had expected to feel, though. But being here was detached from me, as if the whole thing, landing in New York, were happening to someone else. I was but an abstract spectator, a reader perusing a short story.

Gustavo helped me carry my only suitcase out of the Chevy and then upstairs all the way to the fifth floor. The walls were filled with graffiti, obscenities, and lame attempts at drawing cocks and boobs. It wasn't until the next day that the fact that there was no elevator hit me.

Yet it was at that precise moment, as we were going up the filthy stairs, that the notion of having left Mariel behind punched me in the gut. It was a hard blow. My poor daughter was only five. What kind of father leaves his daughter when she's only five? *Those who want a better future for their kids*, my inner voice tried to justify. But that's a false voice. It's the voice one uses to excuse oneself for the shitty and cowardly things one does.

Mariel lived with her mother. We had divorced three years before. I used to think the girl loved me poorly, that her mother had passed (through breast-feeding possibly), the ill-will she'd developed toward me in our rather short marriage. It took me little less than twenty years to accept that such notion was not only ridiculous, but a total fabrication I'd willed myself to believe out of a rotund incapacity to acknowledge my shortcomings as a husband.

It took me that long to understand that failure belonged to the both of us, that neither had been sufficiently in love or even mature enough for marriage.

Isn't that what we do when things don't turn out the way we've planned: blame the other party?

Probably Gustavo noticed my soul had suddenly taken a plunge to a dark place for he jumped into another one of those mile-long monologues that had to do with everything and nothing at the same time. He started on the third floor and didn't stop until we'd dropped the suitcase in my from-that-moment-on room and he'd introduced me to his wife, his two sons, the cat, and a tiny bird with a thousand colors that rested like a queen inside a quite coquettish cage.

The kids' names were Diego and Dylan, eight and nine respectively. They bombarded me with numerous questions that, through nervous grins and weird faces, I tried to ignore.

Dulce (Spanish for Sweet) was Gustavo's wife's name and it was the archetype of the person. She immediately handed me a cup of coffee and whispered, as soon as the others gave her a chance, that I was never to accept a job offer from her husband—for they were never from an honest source. She also gave me permission right then and there to spank the children if they were ever to misbehave with me.

I must have offered her a smile that somehow betrayed the sadness eating my insides because she placed her callous thin hand on my shoulder and said, "Take it easy, chico... you will see everything will be okay."

The next day, at around eight in the morning, after spending four hours turning, tossing, and cursing myself in bed before finally falling asleep and having three nightmares, Gustavo woke me up to tell me he had a job for me.

"*Primo*, get up, I got you a *vainita* with a buddy of mine, an easy couple of bucks. Not a thing to get rich, you know, but better than staying in bed and getting rheum in your eyes."

I remembered Dulce's warning right away but found no reasonable way to refuse Gustavo's offer.

Luckily, right when we were about to leave, Dulce stumbled in with several bags filled with canned food and vegetables. The poor woman was sweating rivers as if she'd just come from the Mojave.

"Oh, you two are up early. What you up to?" She asked amiably, still out of breath, as I gave her a hand with the bags and a look that clearly pleaded for her to save me from Gustavo.

"Nothing, *mujer*, we just going out," he said.

She looked at him up and down and asked him again. This time, she made sure to enunciate both his name *and* last name.

Gustavo had no choice but to tell her we were to meet with *El Maco*, the Frog, who had a painting job for me to make a couple of bucks.

"*El Maco*… are you out of your damn mind, Gustavo? *El Maco*! That scumbag! That's the kind of people you want your cousin hanging out with? You got some balls!"

As soon as she said this, she turned to me and yelled as if I were one of her sons, "You listen carefully, *compai*, if I hear you have set a foot out of this house with this one to do *any* type of work, I'll kick you out like you got lepers. I don't care what it is he says he's getting you. If you are to get a job, it'll be because either you get it yourself or I get it for you."

That statement closed the topic. Gustavo and I stood there, pensive and embarrassed, like two little kids just scolded.

CHAPTER 9

GOOD OLD LIEUTENANT GRANT

In New York, **Ricardo thought,** *we would be dead already.*

"Roberto, let's get out of here. These people won't take long to break in and shower us with bullets. They'll kill us all, son."

Roberto was still behind the column. He was peeking out through the curtains. At his feet, a thousand shards of glass, and, all around him, the collective respiration of everyone gathered there, like the incessant buzz of an AC that's been running the whole night.

The security guard, having grasped the scope of the situation, had opted to remain silent and save his strength.

"Roberto, we must let'em take this man before it's too late," Ricardo told him.

"Let the motherfucker die if it's up to me," he replied.

He suddenly turned around to the women and, pointing at the blonde, told them both, "get up, both of ya, move, now, move!"

Ricardo looked at him.

"Get up, Viejo, move. We're going farther in…"

Ricardo said that wasn't a good idea, assured him the police probably had the building surrounded.

Roberto shook his head and pointed the gun at the old man.

"Move!"

*****

Lieutenant Grant was fifty-two years old and had spent twenty-nine of them in the force. Once and again, his mind used to tell him that he'd seen it all, yet every other day, the streets took it upon themselves to show him how wrong he was, that there was still a lot out there to see, that human stupidity and desperation have no parameters: men compete daily to attain the highest level of absurdity.

Grant was eating a burger when he received the call. He had moved from Chicago to this small town seven years before trying to flee from the busy streets, the vices, the year-long cases, and the violence.

His wife and daughter were content. They didn't care for the smaller house or the school, but did appreciate the long time they now had to share. They also liked the idea of the lieutenant being away from the constantly dangerous streets of Chicago and the sense of peace they found abounded in small-town life. Never before had they had so much time in their hands. And the truth was that sometimes it even felt like it was *just* too much of it.

He had to put the burger away and gulp down the soda. As he drove, he wondered about this guy robbing a bank by himself. The scene seemed so stupid it made him chuckle. Yet, when he arrived, the sergeant confirmed the veracity of the news and added then an aggravating detail: there were hostages.
Grant couldn't believe it. He strode to the front and hid behind one of the cars. He took the loudspeaker and addressed the thief. As he talked into the devilishly loud device, he wondered for the umpteenth time what kind of desperation goes through people's minds to set in motion stupid-ass shit like this.
After a few minutes, there was still no answer. The bank manager (Grant thought he looked old despite his oligarchy-apparent pose) had told him the thief was of Hispanic descent. And young.
Grant nodded. He thought those were the advantages of small towns in contrast to big cities: less pressure, fewer chiefs trying to fuck him up. It translated into more opportunities to get out of that mess without violence... without bloodshed and dead bodies.

Two shots broke him out of that little bubble. Those gathered around the police perimeter ran in all directions.
The agents were alert, somewhat nervous, and awaiting orders.
But Grant said nothing. He did not want an exchange of bullets.

The officers stared at him, incredulous, waiting for his instructions. Grant refused to utter the words.

Something inside told him that giving the order to kill the thief amounted to betraying the life he'd managed to build in that place for his family. It felt like, if he did, he'd be sentencing himself to a fate he had thought eradicated.

He took the loudspeaker and begged for calm. The officers closest to him looked straight at his face. Incredulity masked their countenances.

"What the fuck?" Agent Peña spat out.

Grant ignored him. Neither feelings nor the protection of his ego would interfere with the possibility of preventing a confrontation with the armed robber.

He put the loudspeaker to the side, looked around and, calmly, said:

"There will be no needless loss of blood today, fellas."

CHAPTER 10

SO MUCH FOR THE AMERICAN DREAM

After a month in the city that never sleeps, I still had not found a job. I was desperate.

Back home, Abu no longer produced enough money to support the household. Mami managed a few pesos by washing and ironing other people's clothes, and by selling homemade sweets from an improvised little spot she placed by the entrance door. My sister had a job as secretary for some Realtors, but didn't make much, either. And then there was Mariel with her own needs: food, clothes, school…

That afternoon, it was raining so hard I thought the celestial dams had broken. I was locked in my room with no intention of going out to the living room because outside the moods were acid: Dulce and my cousin had been arguing for the better part of two hours. Real bad arguing. I didn't want to be involved, dragged into the midst of it—each one had been asking me questions with the expectation that I'd speak in their favor, so that they could diss the other one.

According to Dulce, *el primo* had taken some savings she'd hidden in a shoebox. *El primo*, offended, wouldn't have it. They went back and forth calling names, shouting at the top of their lungs, reminding one another of such and such time when you did this or did that. The way they stood in front of one another's face, screaming and gesturing like crazy, made me recall the savage cockfights I witnessed a few times in my trips to Azua.

That's why, I, at the slightest sign of a pause, strode back to my little room. And then I saw the rainfall, like some huge gray cascade threatening to drown the whole world.

The fall of rain often summons an uncommon sense of bitter-sweetness. It is a symbol, a kind of connection between the soul and that element—which pushes us inexorably towards melancholy.

"New York, New York," I said, my voice weary, hoarse, as if I'd been whispering to the time-blackened poster of Billie Jean King on the wall. (More than once I wondered who in that house was a fan of tennis or, if, perhaps, the previous tenants had hung that thing up there and no one, in all these years, had bothered to bring it down.)

"Here, there, anywhere, life's all the same shit if you're just another dot on the endless mass of automaton dots roaming the streets. If you do not know shit, you're shit."

I said this out loud. I wanted my grandfather to hear me say it, to admit defeat for never pursuing the college career he so desperately wanted me to get. I wanted him to hear me say out loud that I had finally wound up the loser he had always feared I would become. Not another second was lost: I wept. That was my first crying session of many in the great city of New York. As I cried, I felt that the connection between my sorrow and the rain grew stronger. As though my loneliness were pouring its own kind of rain inside me—which forced me in time to pour out this torrent of tears.

It would be an understatement to say New York wasn't what I'd been told. There was no money on the sidewalks, life

wasn't easy... not by a long shot. The city wasn't even remotely
the paradise the Dominicanyorks had depicted in their fantastic
yarns of riches, pussy, and luxury. On the contrary, the streets
were ripe with the homeless, especially in the subways, asking for
spare change or food. Some roamed about with their mouths full
with as much filth as their hearts or their clothes.

And the jobs, forget it, the jobs were just too hard to get,
and when you lucked out and found one, the miserable paycheck
didn't last long enough.

Then there was the language, a particularly difficult obstacle. The version of English taught in Dominican technical insti-
tutions, or Learning centers, was not even close to the real thing
spoken (Dare I say "battered"?) in these streets. The lessons from
the *In Tune* and the *Marín Aguilú* were good enough for the island
and to listen to Air Supply songs, but this thing you heard in the
bodegas here was a different thing entirely: the most mundane of
the versions of the language, the most broken. Whoever learned
English back in *el patio* ought to relearn the whole thing here...
from scratch.

At around seven that night, I heard Dulce's tired voice
calling my name, announcing that dinner was ready. When I got
to the dining room, I did not see my *primo* Gustavo. I knew better
than to ask where he was, though. The boys were watching car-
toons: it was about the only time you could count on them to be
quiet.

We ate in silence for about ten minutes. Outside, the rain
had stopped. I imagined for an instant all of the women trotting
their way under awnings and canopies, fleeing from the drizzle
still caressing the streets.

"Your cousin, that damn dog, will no longer be living here," Dulce said, her voice fragile as soap suds. Half a minute passed, in which I entertained myself with a piece of yam in my mouth.

"This is the last time. I told him. I told him I wouldn't stand for his *vagabundería* no more, for all his shit…"

Dulce spoke and chewed at the same time, and the serious face of my grandmother slid through my mind's eye as she scolded me for speaking with my mouth full of food. Hearing her complain, I wondered whether or not that situation would cause me any trouble. Despite my getting along with Dulce, it was Gustavo who happened to be my kin.

She seemed to read my mind for she said, "you worry about nothing. This, mijo, is your home now. Gustavo, he's the spoiled apple in your family."

Dulce was right. Cousin Gustavo was never the meek sheep, but more like the black one. More than once did I hear mami say Gustavo was not *buena cosa*; he was an ungrateful son who never helped his mother—she, who gave him everything. Mom said all he did was spend time with the *tígueres* by the corner and that, surely, he was on drugs, too.

"Tell me who you hang with and I'll tell you who you are," she always said, nodding in agreement to her own wisdom.

In barely a month at that house, I could see for myself that Gustavo wasn't, well, a role model. His time was divided between the couch and the street corner. He had no steady job, but, allegedly, "taxied about" in the Chevy. The truth is I never saw anyone hop into or step out of that car other than *El Maco* or some of the other Dominican and Boricua dudes always by the *bodega*.

"If he knocks and you are here, don't open the door," Dulce sentenced—her eyes fixed on the water streaming down from the faucet.

I was still at the table. She had stood up to wash the dishes. I offered to do it, but, as usual, she refused.

Since I did not acknowledge her order, she turned around and eyed me with severity. I nodded.

"Dulce, were you able to talk to your friend who works with the Italians at the restaurant?" I asked her.

"Yeah, just yesterday. I told him my cousin needs a job and he said he'll speak with the owner because the manager is some cranky old Italian he doesn't like a bit."

After a long silence, she said, "Take it easy. I know what it's like to feel impotent, Ricardo. One way or the other, we all go through this when we first come to New York chasing after the infamous American dream."

"The American dream?" I asked. I had never heard the expression before. Dulce seemed surprised yet non-judgmental.

"The American dream, *mijo*. This, which all of us immigrants do: leaving our homeland to come to the United States hoping to build a better life for ourselves, to try and find here what we couldn't find back home."

She had reclined against the old stove and now tried to wipe her hands dry with some hand towel which, to me, only managed to dirty them up again.

"Wouldn't it be the *Dominican dream* to us then?" I asked, more as a rhetoric question than anything else.

Dulce chuckled and replied that she had never thought about it that way, but, "yeah, to us, it's the Dominican dream, alright… I don't even know why we call it the American dream when it's us, the outsiders, who land here with malformed dreams and wicked hopes based on lies of becoming somebody, of finding the way to send back enough money to put food on the table of our parents and our children, even the husbands and wives we leave behind, stupidly thinking, wishing against all logic, that someday, somehow, we will all be together again as if nothing had happened, as if we hadn't spent five, eight, ten years away from their hugs, their kisses, their tears, and their instances of doubt, of unforgiving loneliness."

She had walked up to the table, almost took a seat but stayed put. "Coffee?" I nodded.
She retraced her steps, found the old coffee maker, and started to get it ready.

"I assume it's because we come to America and America is known as the land of opportunity…" She paused briefly. "Listen to me, fuck, talking like the damn gringos, saying 'America', as if America wasn't the entire continent; as if it was just this one country, this land the white immigrants came to and stole from the natives by way of deceit and bullets. I am a mess, too. I've become part of the problem… Anyways, we want to believe that dreams do come true here…. In the United States of America. We want to believe that, no matter who you are or where you come from, if you have the guts and the will, if you are ready for the sacrifice, here you are destined to triumph…"

I cut her off, "there's no such thing as being *destined to triumph*." The words stumbled out of me much harsher than intended. And with far less hope.

A couple of hours later, already in my room, Dulce's words about the American Dream still resounded in my head.

Why did I come here? I was asked by that voice that is ours yet talks from dark places inside of us. *Abu was right when he said there was nothing here, that it's the same shit everywhere.* I got up from the bed and turned on the television. A white man in his fifties, well-dressed and with an ironic grin, was talking about some fellow by the name of Donald Trump, who had just gifted his fiancé with a 7.5 karat diamond ring worth US$250,000.

Shit! I thought, incredulous. Soon enough, one thought morphed into another and, before I could realize it, I fell asleep. By the time I saw Mariel's face, I had no way to know I was dreaming it.

CHAPTER 11

TOO BIG A CITY TO BE ALONE

It's curious how sometimes people leave things in the hands of time and luck. Not in a procrastinating way but rather a careless one. As if expecting things to resolve themselves, to unfold favorably by the sheer magic of their indifference. It is even more curious when, against all odds and logic, things actually do.

Roberto had no idea what he had gotten himself into when he agreed to travel with Nilo. Only when he got to the airport in Mexico and was about to board the plane to the USA did he ask himself what on earth he was doing. At that moment, all the questions he had failed to ask himself, or Nilo, about their odyssey trampled one another inside his head.

He caught a terrible headache and started to sweat. In no time, he felt everyone around him was eyeing him with inquisitive eyes, especially the security agents at the gate and, later, the immigration officers.

"Bro, what is wrong with you? You were chilling before and now look at you, man. You'll give us away. Stop that shit." Nilo scolded him.

Roberto tried to calm himself down. He tried to convince himself that Nilo knew what he was doing. And so, granting some veracity to those who affirm that ignorance is bliss, they took the plane that would fly them across the ocean and into the land of opportunities.

As soon as the aircraft started its mighty motion upward, Roberto crossed himself and prayed to the good Lord and the Virgin Mary for his life, and for his wife and son.

Nilo, watching him through the corner of his eye, could not hold back a chuckle.

*****

"What is the reason for your visit?" The Border Patrol officer asked Roberto while his gaze alternated between the passport and Roberto's face. Noticing his confusion, the officer, of oriental traits, asked him in quite a rudimentary Spanish, "Qué razón… visit… visitor… visitando… Estades Unides?"

Roberto felt the first droplets of sweat forming on his neck and forehead. He had always hated how his body reacted to stress: by perspiring uncontrollably—like some damaged appliance.

He did not understand what the officer was saying. English was still an unknown forest full of dangerous sounds and noises. However, Nilo had instructed him on what questions he might be asked, had even written down some examples on a piece of paper, along with what to answer. Things like, 'visiting friends', some names, telephone numbers, and addresses, that Roberto memorized —he thought— but could no longer remember.

"De paseo," he said.

"Pa – so?" the officer asked, his face denoting doubt.

"No… um... pa-se-ou, visitando… a-mi-gous,"

Roberto tried to clarify his words in that annoying Dominican habit (when talking to a native English speaker) of splitting words into syllables and pronouncing them in what we *think* are "English sounds."

The officer, realizing this could take much longer than he had wished for, gestured for Roberto to stay put and be quiet. He closed the passport, inched half his torso (turtle-like) outside his booth, and looked everywhere. After a minute, it seemed like he couldn't find whoever he was looking for and repositioned himself on the seat.

Exhaling deeply, he took a glimpse at the line that awaited him. It was getting longer by the minute.

He resumed the perusing of the passport and papers before him. After a few verifications and notations, he signaled for Roberto to place his finger on a tiny glass scanner for fingerprints.

Roberto didn't move. His nerves wouldn't allow him. He didn't even try to move his finger in the direction of the little red light that awaited like a laser beam ready to amputate his limbs.

The officer had to hold each one of Roberto's fingers and place them one by one on the scanner until the whole procedure was finally completed.

Roberto's countenance remained dumb-struck. The officer then pointed at a camera lens on a tripod. "Here," he said, visibly annoyed, as he pointed repeatedly with his long lean finger. Before Roberto could position himself comfortably in front of the camera, the officer snapped the photo, stamped the passport, and shooed Roberto away.

"Go in, go in, sir," he repeated, with uncontrollable exasperation. Unbeknownst to him, his clumsiness and ignorance of the English language had indirectly granted him access to the most secure immigration system in the world.

From the Baggage Claim area, just behind a tall glass wall, Nilo grinned with relief.

"Eso fue migración, loco. Ahora falta aduana. Cógelo suave que aquí cualquiera nos devuelve," Nilo said. He explained that things were different here: they had gone through Immigration and now had to go through Customs—anybody could kick them back to their country for any reason they deemed pertinent.

"Eyes wide open, bro," he said.

Roberto said yes with little conviction. He felt lost inside that humongous dimension of white walls, shiny handrails, people of all shapes and sizes, dressed in their Sunday's best, checking on their top-of-the-line cell phones, glimpsing at expensive watches, listening attentively to the announcements from the speakers or picking up their luggage from a winding conveyor belt.

The line to get to the Customs officers was quite long. As they inched closer, their nerves rattled like deadly copperheads—Nilo thought he was coping with his nerves better than Roberto did. The truth was there wasn't a clear difference: they were both looking here and there, everywhere. Evidently restless.

When Roberto finally reached the officer, he asked for his passport and tickets, the ones used to identify the luggage. He asked Roberto what the purpose of his visit was and, once again, Roberto remained mute, with a question mark decorating his face.

This time around, though, the officer, despite his utterly Yankee appearance, addressed him in fluid Spanish and, if Roberto read him right, an expression of doubt on his face…

"Mexicano?" He asked while his left hand waved the passport lightly up and down as if trying to guess its weight.

"Sí."

The man eyed him in silence for seconds that lasted way too long.

"¿Y qué viene a hacer a los Estados Unidos, caballero?" Roberto hesitated for only a tenth of a second. He'd been asked the reason for his visit before, all he had to do was say what Nilo had told him.

"Ah, eh, vengo a visitar a uno amigo mío," he said finally, lying about visiting friends.

"Y esos amigos, ¿dónde viven?"

"En el Bronx…"

"En el Bronx, jum, Okay… So, ¿usted es mexicano? Porque… usted me parece dominicano."

For this question, he did have an answer. Nilo had warned him that they might suspect he had not been born in Mexico. The response would be that he had naturalized Mexican years earlier. His mom had been Mexican. They had certified papers for every one of these claims. The officer did not even blink as he heard the explanation. His gut told him Roberto was lying, but the paperwork was legit.

"¿Tiene usted la dirección de su amigo? El Bronx es bastante grande."

Roberto sensed two things: first, that this dude was no idiot and, second, that, if he remained calm, this man might just let him go.

So, he made a herculean effort to seem nonchalant and normal about not knowing this address by heart. He told the officer he had it somewhere in his suitcase and looked at him like they were cousins or something. He even called him *'mi hermano,'* like they were close friends who'd lost contact and fate had just reunited them.

The officer eyed him for a full three seconds, up and down—an almost imperceptible grin on his lips.

"Come with me, manito, venga," he told him with a mixture of amusement and duty.

He took him a good fifty meters away to a metallic table and asked him (in that subtle yet authoritative tone we all know is a command disguised as a request) to please place the suitcase on top of the table and open it.

"¿Tiene usted algo que declarar?" he asked in that perfect Spanish of his. And yet, Roberto did not understand the question. He thought the officer, by using the expression 'anything to declare?', meant drugs. But he knew better than to mention it without being sure, so he just asked what he meant.

The officer said he meant food, alcohol, money, or live animals. Roberto was so surprised at the variety that he let out a loud chuckle and immediately apologized.

"No, no traigo na de eso, jefe, no."
"Muy bien, voy a revisar su equipaje. Ponga atención, por favor."

Roberto nodded but, from the get-go, he wasn't paying attention at all. He was looking at Nilo, who was at another table, two hundred meters away. The agent with him didn't seem too talkative. Nilo was taking small steps in the same spot, looking everywhere and talking more than necessary.

"Sir?" The agent's voice brought him back to his situation.

"Here are your documents. Have a good time in the land of dreams."

He handed Roberto his passport and, smiling almost mischievously, motioned for him to leave.

Roberto did not understand what he was being told, but it was clear that the man had just welcomed him into the United States.

When Roberto reached the exit, he had the instinct to wait for Nilo, but, as he turned around, he saw the agent still staring at him.

He also saw Nilo. He had just been surrounded by three more officers and was shaking his head.

The people behind Roberto had to walk around him. As they passed, they looked at him with annoyed expressions.

Roberto had to move forth toward the exit—not knowing what would happen to his cousin.

*****

An hour went by and there was no sign of Nilo. Every five minutes, some Dominican man would approach him to ask if he needed a taxi.

There were also African taxi drivers who said, "Papi, taxi, papi?" And Roberto shook his head as he kept his gaze fixed on the corridor where he had cleared Customs. Nothing. The passengers on the flight from Mexico were already gone. The monitors announced the arrival of passengers on a flight from Puerto Rico and another one from Panama.

Roberto didn't know what to do. He and Nilo never pondered the possibility of Nilo being stopped and not him. Now he was in New York, alone, without a cell phone, without relatives or friends. Nilo had been his only contact and his only plan.

He reached into his pockets and pulled out a handful of dollars. Counted them calmly. Two hundred and forty-two. Roberto had no idea how much money that was in this country where everything seemed inaccessible, modern, and out of reach.

He put his right hand on his head and wondered about his future out loud, "Coño, Roberto... ¿y ahora?"

CHAPTER 12

POE'S PLACE AND A DERANGED BOSS

I arrived on 84th street at around 9:00 a.m. Dulce had told me that the place opened at 10:00 a.m., but it was wise to arrive early both to make a good impression and to have enough time in my favor in case I got lost.

It was the first time in a month and a half in New York that I went out by myself. The other two or three times I'd left the apartment had been to go to the Deli or to the supermarket, which were just three or four blocks away.

Dulce had managed to get me a job in the kitchen of Edgar's Cafe restaurant, where a friend of hers worked. Edgar's Cafe was some kind of historical site. It was located on 84th Street, in the Brennen Mansion, where for a year, from 1844 to 1845, poet Edgar Allan Poe had lived.

Dulce had given me ten dollars and made me a small bag with bread and cheese and mayonnaise, and two pretty ripe *guineos*. She wrote down her friend's phone number and the restaurant's and gave me five quarters in case I got lost and had to use a public phone. And tokens, too, for the train.

Twenty minutes after my arrival, a short stocky gentleman arrived, who seemed to me to be of Mexican descent. Without saying hello, he climbed the steps, pushed the door open, and rushed in.

For a few minutes, I debated whether or not I should do the same, but right when I had made up my mind, a young woman—who also seemed Mexican to me—came and did the same: she went up, pushed the door open, and entered. Before disappearing, though, she turned around and asked me in Spanish if I needed help. "Yes, thank you, me new to work… here… and I… begin at ten in morning. I talk to Danny." She nodded in understanding –suppressing laughter– and gestured for me to enter.

The place was quite nice. There was a large mahogany counter with several rows of crystalline, shiny glasses. Behind it, a sophisticated and apparently complicated coffee-brewing machine, a shelf full of liquor bottles, and a display case with various desserts. There was an ivory white telephone, several plates, knives, and forks arranged neatly in a kind of drawer or tray, a few rolls of coins, and a vertical lamp. On the right-hand side was the entrance to the kitchen and on the left, the entrance to the main room, where all the tables were set. The decor was wine-colored with hints of gold and orange brushstrokes. There was a painting of a crow, which I later learned was in honor of one of Poe's most famous poems; and a caricature of the poet's face, with a brief inscription underneath.

The Mexican girl motioned for me to enter the kitchen with her. There was the Mexican I'd seen before and another man, older, of an elusive aspect, white hair, matching beard, and small and cunning eyes—the constantly-scrutinizing type.

The young woman greeted them good morning. The Mexican smiled and nodded. The other one, whom I assumed was Danny, responded in serious, heavily-accented English, with the same words. Then he looked at me and asked me in English who I was.

I wanted to answer, but I wasn't sure what the man had said. That's how complicated his accent was—and how poor my English.

Since I did not respond, the young woman asked me my name. "Oh… uh… my name is Ricardo," I said... with inexplicable fear.

Danny said a few things to the young woman and she replied. They both looked at me and then at each other. There was a weird grin on Danny's face. I thought then they were perhaps talking about my poor English, but over time I sensed they were just making fun of my moron face.

Danny told me (in what I understood then was a mixture of Spanish, Italian and English) that my job would be to help José, the Mexican, in the kitchen. He said he would pay me US$5.00 an hour and that I'd work six days a week. My day off would be Tuesday. I wanted to thank him, but he put an apron on the counter and told me to get to work.

José and María turned out to be two extremely pleasant, funny and hard-working fellows. They patiently taught me the ten thousand things that had to be learned in that infernal kitchen, from washing dishes with gloves on ("Hey, your fingers are going to rot if you don't put them on, guey!"), cutting vegetables with a huge knife, cleaning the shrimp's bottom ("See that little black thingy there, guey? That's the shit of the fucking shrimp!"), to tying knots with a rope around the discarded-to-be cardboard boxes.

They tried to teach me words in a nice indigenous dialect, which I never learned. They told me their stories: how they had crossed the border, how María's sister had betrayed her by fucking María's husband in the house that María had built with the money she sent... I told them about Abu and the trip. I told them they were the only people I had spoken to in that entire month. These things happened in just three days.

The storage room was on the left side of the building. You had to go out on the sidewalk, open the padlock on the fence, go down the stairs and walk a hundred feet to get to that cold room. You had to use different keys to unlock the door and then hook the door to the wall to avoid getting trapped inside. It was a large room where every half hour or so you had to go in to get napkins, eggs, cheese, flour, oil... Everything was arranged in an order impossible to guess in three or four days.

At about seven o'clock on the evening of the fourth day, Danny told me to get trash bags. I went downstairs immediately, but lost two to three minutes debating on which ones to bring, as there were five different types and the boss hadn't specified which. When I finally got out (carrying two packages of each), I saw Danny waiting for me on the sidewalk. One more step and the man started screaming at the top of his lungs: "What you doing down there so long? What you stealing? You fucking thief!"

Of the three or four sentences Danny yelled (which I have pieced together in my memory over and over again in an attempt to grasp the full scope of his disrespect), the only thing I clearly understood was the word *Thief*.

I felt so much anger and humiliation that my tongue got stuck, and of everything I wanted to say to him, I only managed to shout in Spanglish: "Thief are you, *maricón*!"

He must have realized how angry I was, for he immediately returned to the restaurant. I followed him all the way to the counter and, once there, threw the bags at his feet.

"I am not thief! You more thief then me!" I yelled at him in my broken English and at the top of my lungs. The wretched Italian was as red as a Caribbean pepper.

"Shut up, shut up!" He yelled back a couple of times, but I ignored him. I screamed at him. My Spanish filling every poetic corner of the mansion where the Brenners had once surely had their tea and taken their wealthy-ass shits in clean white toilets, and where ravens had taken flight every night from Poe's slim fingers.

I screamed all the curse words I could muster. And when I thought I was about to have a heart attack, the guy pulled out forty dollars from under the counter and slapped them on the countertop. "Take your money and no come back!" He screamed like a mad man.

I didn't even touch the money. I gestured for him to pick it up. Told him in Spanish (although he clearly didn't understand a single word) that he needed the money more than I did. I took off my dirty apron, looked at José and María (who stared at me with a mixture of amazement and pity), and left.

Two days later, sitting at the table with Dulce, with not a single dollar in my possession, I still felt so much rage and helplessness that two tears slipped down my cheeks like two little marbles.

"What is it, muchacho? You can't pay no mind to that shit. Those Italian motherfuckers are racists; don't listen to them. Is there a single human being more corrupt than them damn Italians? Shiit!"

I had to laugh. I'd never met another Italian before this crazy-ass Danny, but if one were to believe the representations of films or books, it would have to be concluded they were all charming, stylish gangsters.

I took a sip of coffee and we remained silent for a few minutes. Outside, the city seemed to argue with itself: the noises that reached us were impossible to pinpoint; and yet, they were the precise dialect of all streets, with their cacophony of people, screeching trains, sudden horns, music, and sirens. I thought about how different my street was from these streets full of hustle at all hours, but immediately corrected myself, because the hustle and bustle of the streets are always the same, what varies is the intensity. These streets in the Bronx were intense. Not everyone knew what was happening or how, but the men in the corners passing 'things' from hand to hand, and the shootings that were already commonplace, gave a clear idea that things were not going too well.

Dulce took a final sip and said, "to think you left that motherfucker your forty dollars!"

We both laughed.

CHAPTER 13

THEY WILL KILL US ALL

Roberto ordered them to go in the manager's office. Ricardo thought it a bad idea, but Roberto was desperate and wasn't listening.

Though strong, the Security guard had lost too much blood and Ricardo started to fear the worst. He was also confused by Lieutenant Grant's attitude. He had yet to give the order to enter and get rid of the threat. It was an unexpected, but welcome truce.

The women went in first. Right after, with great effort, Ricardo managed to move the security guard and place him in a chair. Roberto closed the door, locked it from the inside. He went to the phone and sat down in front of it, placing the two duffel bags with the money next to the desk. Instinctively, he rubbed his wounded leg while resting his forehead on his right hand. The gleaming black pistol barely a foot from his face. After a few seconds, he said:

"When I got here, the airport people detained my cousin Nilo, who'd brought me over..." said Roberto, his voice muffled by exhaustion.

"What happened?" Ricardo asked. He knew Roberto was talking to him.

"They deported him. That same day."

In the silence of the office, the breathing of the five was like being among the dying in an asylum. Fleetingly, Ricardo remembered Darth Vader and the entertained face of his daughter—who had watched The Return of the Jedi with him without really understanding it. In other circumstances, sure enough, he would have smiled.

"Since that day, the only thing I've done here is struggle and be angry. I am tired. I'm tired of so much fucking around to get nothi…" He paused and let out a sigh.

Roberto then thought about his mother. For reasons he would never get to grasp, he remembered the afternoon she took him to *el malecón*. He must have been eight, maybe nine years old. They walked for a while, at intervals on the grass and the wide boardwalk. To their right, the beach that people called *Güibia* stretched for miles on end. It seemed to open up as wide as the sky itself to welcome the vast green-blue sea that, almost magically, touched and melted into the horizon. All alongside the boardwalk, there were vendors, some in parked vans and trucks, others in tricycles. There were lovers sitting on stone benches and young people jogging. Other children, younger than him, ran around a tree trying to catch or tap one another. He noticed an old man sitting on one of the farther, bigger rocks, beyond the boardwalk, in an area that seemed dangerous, where nobody else seemed eager to step into. He looked back at his mom and smiled. She bought him ice cream from a street vendor: chocolate and vanilla. They stood a moment later by some musicians singing and playing the guitar for a group of older people at a table. Everyone was in a good mood. A lady, as old as his grandmother, wearing a beautiful yellow dress, stood up, right next to the singers, and started to sing, too. She had the voice of an angel. Roberto remembered how happy his mom had seemed then, how unburdened and young and full of life. One of the men, with a light-blue shirt and a hat, stood up as well and asked another lady to dance. And dance they did, slowly and joyfully, at the cadence and rhythm of the song in the melodious voices of the street singers and the nice lady in the yellow dress. And everyone laughed a tender laughter and smiled as if nothing could ever again go wrong in the entire world.

"I came here to do whatever it takes to get my boy and my wife a better life... and so that I could get enough money to pay someone... to kill that son of a bitch."

Ricardo glanced at him. Roberto suddenly looked much older.

"Kill who? Your cousin?" He asked.

Roberto shook his head. He was silent then for a minute, maybe two.

"Everyone has both an angel and a demon in their life to accompany them, *primo*. My mother was my angel and my pai... My fucking father... he *is* my demon. That animal killed my mother. Because of him, I am in this life. I will not rest until I see him dead."

It sounded like the apocalypse of the scriptures had started. Everyone shook out of suddenness and fear. Roberto took the gun and went to the women right away, who screamed their lungs out.

The police were inside the bank. There was a chorus of footsteps, the peculiar sound of various bodies moving with agility and caution, the crystalline wailing of glass broken under rushing boots.

If Ricardo wanted to say something, he did not dare. Roberto was holding the blonde by the hair, using her as a human shield. He motioned for the brunette to grab the two loot bags.

The security guard watched the scene with a sort of dark resignation in his clouded pupils. Nerves threatened to wreak havoc on everyone. And it was justified: if the police were inside, it meant the order to attack had been given.

Roberto and Ricardo looked at each other briefly. But that fleeting contact was enough to comprehend that nobody would likely get out of there alive.

*****

Lieutenant Grant had given the order. The thief had shown no signs of wanting to surrender, his men were nervous and, to top it all, there was already a dozen television cameras on the scene. Someone, as usual, would soon question why a rescue mission had not yet been attempted, and others would echo.

In less than an hour, his name would be on Twitter and Instagram: trending.

It was Ricardo who noticed there was another door.

Outside the office, the policemen had already positioned themselves and were ready to go in and spread lead. One of them, with a boyish voice, had just yelled at Roberto to surrender, told him he was surrounded. Said it in Spanish, too.

Ricardo imagined him in his uniform, with his protective helmet, kevlar vest, and boots tied up almost to the knee, like the old Roman Coliseum fighters. He imagined him to be in his mid-twenties, Honduran perhaps by his accent, with the rifle or sub-machine gun in his hands, ready to take Roberto's life.

But Ricardo knew that, to kill Roberto, the chances of them getting killed as well were just too high.

So, instinctively (desperately), he looked for some way to get out of there. It was then that he saw the door, at the end of a narrow hallway (that would lead them first to a kitchen and then to a small bathroom). A door barely distinguishable from the wall.

Ricardo pointed at the door. He signaled at Roberto, so that he would look down the narrow hall and see it. Roberto was sweating in spurts, his hand clenching tightly against the blonde's hair—who kept crying.

The brunette was sobbing in a corner, holding the heavy money bags as if they were her dear children.

Roberto moved a little forward to see what Ricardo was trying to show him. When he saw the door, he didn't think twice about it and, pushing the blonde, motioned for the others to move to the hallway.

Ricardo looked and pointed at the security guard, and shook his head: implying that it was impossible to carry him. Roberto nodded.

Ricardo and the brunette entered the hall, followed by the blonde and Roberto, leaving the wounded guard behind.

The police again asked Roberto to turn himself in, clarified that he had nowhere to go, and ordered him to release the hostages.

Ricardo was convinced that they'd soon break down the door and start spraying them with bullets like some lethal irrigation system.

The brunette tried the knob, the door was locked. Ricardo turned to look at Roberto and shook his head. Roberto cursed under his breath.

He pushed the blonde toward the others and returned to the office. The security guard seemed asleep or dead. Blood had long ago soaked the piece of shirt Ricardo had tied around the wound and was now painting everything at his feet a dark blobby red.

Roberto rummaged among the drawers in the desk. Nothing. He heard movements behind the door, told himself that the police were ready to enter. He thought his only way out would be to break down the other door and try to escape from behind. When he was about to do it, his peripheral vision saw the shape of a keychain hooked to a jacket on the back of a chair. His eyes lit up. He took the keys and ran to the others.

He realized he was limping. The adrenaline had muffled the pain from the wound in his leg so far, but he was still losing blood and it was already taking its toll. He handed the key ring to Ricardo and looked back: just then the other door jumped off its hinges with a rain of splinters.

From where they were, they could see the metal head of the tool the police had used to break in: it looked like a huge steel dildo. Then they saw two policemen in black uniforms and protective helmets enter—their long weapons before them.

Roberto fired first: once, twice, three times. The cops had hoped to meet him head-on, not on the right flank. They all backed out as fast as they'd entered. The door hung in an almost funny position, like a drunkard about to fall, who'd managed to prevent it by some miraculous grace of a divine nature.

Roberto shouted in his broken 'hood Spanish, "*Vamo, vamo,*" and he, Ricardo, the blonde and the brunette managed to get to the other side before the roar of the gunshots silenced all the other noises. Roberto shot at them again while running to save his life. He tried to close the door behind him, but knew they had to keep running because that wouldn't stop the assailants.

The room they found was dark. It was some type of warehouse. Looking everywhere, Ricardo wondered what the hell the architect who designed the place had been smoking.

CHAPTER 14

GIRO O ROLO

Roberto, who had been waiting for Nilo for over three hours, finally gave up and approached one of the Dominican taxi drivers—told him he had nowhere to go. He then asked him to take him somewhere to spend the night.

"*Y donde hablen español.*"

"*Tranquilo, primo,*" the cab driver replied, "you're in good hands."

He helped him load the suitcases and took him to the upper Manhattan. Charged him US$70.00. "That trip is almost a hundred dollars, *primo, pero usted es dominicano y hay que echarle una manito,*" he assured him it was a fair price.

The taxi left him in front of an aging building with a battered MOTEL sign. He helped him unload the suitcases and, before leaving, warned him in Spanish to keep his eyes open, for the area was not particularly good.

The motel stairs were the steepest Roberto had ever seen in his life. It took him three full minutes to bring the first suitcase up. When he went back down to get the other one, out of sheer rage, he almost had a heart attack: it was not there.

Roberto stepped out to the sidewalk. No sign of the suitcase. A couple passed by, kissing. On the opposite sidewalk, several people were walking hurriedly. He looked everywhere, incredulous, embarrassed, and boiling-blood angry. "*Hijos de la gran
puta*," he cursed with a grunt.

He jogged back up, cursing under his breath, and felt like
he was climbing the Everest.

At the counter, a man in his early sixties with a profuse
mustache and a four-day-old beard looked at him and waved re-
luctantly. Roberto told him he needed a room and the man (who
understood enough Spanish as to not ask again) asked him for
identification and $25.00 to stay the night.

Roberto showed the man his passport and gave him the
money. The man scrutinized him and his identification more me-
ticulously than the immigration agent had.

Finally, as if it were the normal thing to do, he asked
Roberto what was in the suitcase. Roberto, not expecting such a
question, answered with one of the few English words he remembered, "My shirt," and the man nodded as if that were the only
reasonable answer.

The clerk handed him a key linked to an aluminum chain
and said, "102."

Since Roberto didn't move, the grumpy old man pointed
at the hallway and, with an up-and-down motion of his wrist, ur-
ged him to go, like someone trying to get rid of a child who won't
stop fooling around.

The room had a bed, a nightstand with a drawer, a vertical mirror leaning against the wall, a small bathroom, a closet with

seven or eight hangers, and a television set of a brand that started with the letter K—which Roberto had never heard of.

The bed was done but the sheets seemed tanned either by excessive use or people's overall dirt.

Roberto threw himself on it anyway, put his arms behind his neck, and tried to fall asleep. But sleep did not come immediately. Instead, he wondered what the hell he would do without Nilo, without money, without knowing anyone. Just like back in prison, he felt helpless.

His mom's face came to him and his eyes filled with imminent tears. He wiped them away with his forearm, took a deep breath, and reproached himself: "*Maricón*, men don't cry!"

After a while, he fell asleep. When he opened his eyes, he realized that he'd slept through the entire night. He had the feeling that he had dreamed of something, although he couldn't remember what.

The morning, which took over the little room, gave him new energy. He stood up ready to bathe and go out, see to what he would do. "You have to go out there and find a life. You're here now, you have to get your ass ready." He said out loud.

Then his father's face flashed through his mind as a reminder of why he was in that situation. He shook his head. While undressing, he thought that he might check the area since it was evident there were many Dominicans around. He had come to this conclusion for three reasons: the taxi driver took him there, the old man at the counter spoke Spanish, and the sign said Motel. (He had no way to know the word is written the same way in both languages.)

Everything is simple when you know how to do it. When you have never done something, no matter how easy, the first attempt is always complicated.

Roberto faced a shower for the first time in his life in that motel room. Back in DR, bathing consisted of water in a bucket, a bar of soap (of a kind people called *jabón de cuaba*), and a *morrito*—a small plastic container to pour the water on you. Even after he started dealing drugs and making money, he never gave himself the chance of discovering what a shower was (or anything else, for that matter) like some of the other dudes did by taking girls they met at the clubs to the motels and the *cabañas*. He had simply been too focused to fool around, too angry to care about anything other than his revenge and his money schemes.

So, he looked at the long giraffe-like neck of the shower and the rusty head as if they were extraterrestrial. The three knobs at his thighs' height seemed to challenge him. He looked everywhere: in the bathtub, along the sides of the toilet, behind the door... looking for a hose, a bucket, or a bowl, but there was none of that. It was just he and that long, strange, nickel-plated artifact.

Out of pure instinct, he reached for the knob on the right, turned it just so. Nothing. He tried the middle one but was so unsure of what he was doing he just tapped on it. Then he tried the one on the left. This one, perhaps because he was already frustrated, he turned hard. A stream of freezing water came down on him. It was so cold, he wanted to scream. But he had no time: almost right away, the water went from ice-cold to hell-hot. This boiling water leaped out of the showerhead like a volcano spewing lava. Roberto jumped three, four, five times inside the tub, desperately trying to evade the liquid fire that threatened to burn his genitals. As he could, he blindly reached for the knob on the right and turned it, then the middle one, meanwhile, without realizing it, he kept shouting: "*Ay, mierda, coño, diablo, me quemo*!"

When he left the room, the man with the profuse mustache was not there. In his place, there was a woman in her late twenties, whom Roberto deemed 'extraordinarily ugly', filing her nails as she spoke (in English) on her cell phone. She looked him up and down and resumed her chat. Roberto walked down the kilometer-long stairs, came to the sidewalk, and seemed to him he had landed in another world. He couldn't determine how many people there were. For a moment, he was undecided on which way to walk, right or left, but then he thought it was all the same because he had no point of reference: he was going to an uncertain destination anywhere he chose.

He took the first step and then allowed himself to be led by the stream of people in that direction. As he walked, he observed everything around him. He could not help feeling that he was in the corner of Duarte Avenue and Paris Street, back in DR, due to the crowd, the variety of stores, the humid heat, and the vendors of pork rinds and fresh juice in the corners.

Impossible for him to imagine that New York would be this: this gigantic version of the streets of Santo Domingo. A couple of realities assailed him then: the understanding that in New York people spoke more Spanish than English, and the disappointment that it was not remotely the fantastic, clean, and imposing city of stories and movies.

As he walked, he looked up for the skyscrapers but saw none. He wondered where in the big city they were and even began to doubt their existence.

He stood in front of a Deli that advertised in vivid colors a menu of assorted sandwiches. His stomach said something in the universal language of hunger and he walked in. After a minute of hesitation, he ordered a ham-and-cheese sandwich.

The clerk, whose cap showed an embroidered Dominican flag, asked him, "*Giro o Rolo, primo?*" Roberto did not understand the question, so he answered, "*No, manin, jamón y queso.*"

A man in his sixties looked at him and laughed out loud.

"You just came from *el patio, verdad?*" The clerk asked him. Roberto, a little upset and a little embarrassed, told him he didn't speak English yet, and the man, nodding and smiling, replied, "*así llegamos todos, primo. Sin saber de na. Bievenido a la jungla de acero.*" And then he repeated in English, not really knowing why: "Welcome to the jungle of steel." With the same friendly smile, he explained the difference between the *Giro* (hero) and the *Rolo* (roll). Roberto decided on the first one.

While waiting, he asked the nice gentleman if he knew of anyone who was hiring. The old man who'd mocked him before looked him up and down and made a face.

The clerk said he did not. A few minutes later, he handed Roberto his food. He suggested that maybe Roberto should walk a couple of blocks down to the barbershops. Perhaps, they were hiring. Roberto paid and thanked him.

As he was leaving, he overheard the old man say, "Can you believe this *tecato*, Bolivar? A job! This rat's looking for a drug point."

Roberto needed no English to know the old man was talking shit about him; felt like turning around and letting the old fart have it, but decided against it. The truth was the old man was probably right. He had not traveled to New York to pretend to be an exemplary citizen but to get rich. He knew the only way to get rich was by hustling.

And although he figured it would not be the same as back on the island, he also knew what he had to do to start the business.

What he didn't have was time. That complicated things for him. So, he walked for a while, four, five blocks, corner to corner, as covertly as possible. He located four groups of drug dealers in different corners. Three of the groups were mixed. Only the farthest one was made up exclusively of blacks. He reckoned the blacks might be the only ones working for a differ-rent provider.

CHAPTER 15

ANOTHER BAD JOB

Regal Prestige was the name of the high-quality pressure cooker company where Dulce got me a job as a salesperson. She spoke with some dude by the name of Leonel, an acquaintance of hers, who had been in the business for many years and who, as he said when she introduced us (not short on drama and arrogance), was already at a level of absolute comfort, "on the verge of financial freedom."

That term, 'Financial Freedom', would become, from then on, the anthem and motto, goal and base, ideal and chimera, of all my days and the days of those who, like me, entered this maze-like world of prospecting and seducing potential buyers into getting a set of pots and pans.

Leonel was unable to say seven words in a row without mentioning Financial Freedom. It was like a mantra, almost a crutch, repeated over and over without regard, sometimes even without coherence. Talking to him was more like taking (recurrently and non-stop) an intensive course on sales strategies, tips for evaluating prospects (potential clients), and methods to refute objections... the thousand and one ways to achieve Financial Freedom: that holy grail of the pot dealer (no pun intended.)

Leonel feigned charming honesty. He spoke of his beginnings, of having given up good jobs for the opportunity to leave the modern slavery of arbitrary hours and little time for the family; of having seen beyond a salary that would never be enough to get him even close to his dreams; of grasping that beautiful, mysterious, and attainable thing (in little over five or six years)—we already know, right?—Financial Freedom.

He had the easy verb of priests and the grace of a movie star. He always dressed in a suit and tie and enjoyed cooking and whiskey. He was overloaded with self-esteem and never took no for an answer. When we took rides in his car, we listened, without pause or fail, to the manly voice of brother Leonel, who recited various variations of the same sermon to us. Leonel knew how to sell the dream of Financial Freedom like no other.

But selling it and reaching it were two different things. Regal Prestige's specialty was the selling of pots, cookers, pans, water filters, and other kitchen utensils of the highest quality... and at the most exorbitant prices. Hence the difficulty of selling the products. They were so expensive that a credit check and approval process had to be done for potential customers, who, if approved, had to finance the products. They were one thousand and two-thousand-dollar cookware sets. Of course, with a lifetime guarantee.

I remember I put on a pale, yellow shirt, a tie I borrowed from Gustavo's closet (Gustavo was still missing in action), and went to the Regal Prestige offices for my first day of work at about eight twenty in the morning. One by one, the others arrived, too. In total, we were five new recruits and four old souls.

Leonel introduced us as if he'd known us all his life. He highlighted characteristics and qualities of each one of us that we ourselves did not know we possessed. At the end of the meeting, we all felt more capable than when we'd arrived. Leonel had filled us with endless possibilities. In this man's head, everything about our future appeared to be quite clear, although we were unable to fully understand how or believe it.

Thereafter, we were "fortunate" to discover and be acquainted with a broad amalgam of "accomplished" personalities who met in the office every week, and who recounted impressive stories of success, travel, and, of course, financial freedom to do what they wanted, when they wanted.

Some, I noticed, were careful to be the last to enter and the first to leave (I eventually concluded they did not want us to see their second-class cars or, worse, to see them walk towards the bus or the train), while others, always the same—one whom they dubbed The Doctor and another, The Master—remained till the very end of the meetings with the almost brazen purpose of showing off for the newcomers their newly purchased (leased?) vehicles.

As in all businesses where you talk about residual income, not being slaves to a job, being your own boss, reaching a point—in a relatively short time—where you can stop working in order to enjoy the honey of your efforts, and the apparent ease with which these things are accomplished, what never fails is the fact that in a pretty short time you get to discover the incongruous details. That is to say, the reality that was lived daily at work did not agree with the theory: the people who'd already been there for quite some time were still in the same situation of poverty as those who had just arrived, the leaders were not inordinately better, sales numbers did not match odds, and, day in and day out, there was much more expectation than action.

As an old Dominican adage goes: the issue with Regal Prestige was nothing but "make-belief and aimless-motion." In other words: act like you are getting rich and pretend you are really busy making moves.

The leaders of our Regal prestige circle painted a bright picture, but when we were out on the streets for ten hours straight standing in parks, on sidewalks, under the cold or the scorching sun; when we stopped people on Fordham Road to ask them if they were interested in cookers a thousand dollars each and their eyes alone threatened to murder us right then and there; when we entered buildings to knock on doors (in clear violation of the laws that, I learned later, prohibit what Americans call Soliciting), or when we had to mobilize and did not even have a MetroCard for the train—because in two months we still had not made a single sale—the painting these assholes had created for us had no brightness whatsoever, but a gloomy layer of despair and disappointment.

The *ñapa*, the last straw, was the day good old Leonel invited us to his house to meet a certain Jorge Lantigua, Gold Diamond Platinum Deluxe Executive, or some such ridiculous title: one of those conceived to dazzle—appealing to the vanity of the unwary.

The good sir, who had just turned 35, was already, according to Leonel, the youngest millionaire in the astounding history of Regal Prestige, earning the stratospheric sum of no less than US$100,000 a month—I still remember my amazement and incredulity when Leonel mentioned that amount.

I cannot deny, however, having been somewhat curious. It takes little for the desperate to find hope, even in words they know carry no sense. But hope, well, hope feeds off itself. So, I admit to nesting a poor little hope that this guy might show us something, anything, that would justify our time there.

It didn't happen.

The only positive thing about this meeting was that it represented the forceful and final blow that would positively end my frustrating relationship with that business once and for all.

The millionaire was six feet six inches tall, with a fair complexion and sad eyes. He looked young, but his was a tired youth; and when he smiled, there was no joy in his smile, just a kind of customary civility... and something tattooed by force of repetition, very likely the habit, or the inertia, of lying.

In an inconceivable act of humility, the millionaire preferred to spend the night in a tiny bed in Leonel's living room than to go to a fancy, comfortable hotel. When we went to lunch, he preferred to go with us, cramped in Leonel's vehicle, rather than rent one or even take a taxi. Despite having so much money, the good millionaire did not even once attempt to pay for the meals of those of us who accompanied him. Leonel paid for everything.

At the end of that day, I looked at Leonel in the eye and said, "Thank you, brother, but this shit is not for me."

CHAPTER 16

SEE YA, LUV

"Shit!" Roberto said in a low voice. He was sitting on the edge of the bed counting a few bills. He'd been trying to ration the money, but after two weeks of paying for the motel, he didn't have much left. Getting into the drugs business had proved much more difficult than he'd imagined. His willingness to risk it all, even his life, was not enough. Back in el patio, it was all about having *cojones*, putting your foot down, and investing a couple of thousand pesos. There was no organization, no hierarchy whatsoever. You had the merch and the balls to shoot some motherfucker, you were king of the jungle. Here, Roberto realized soon enough, having balls amounted to shit.

On the wall, next to the TV, a tiny cockroach paced as if in a recreational field. He watched it for a long time. He thought dimly that *he* too was a cockroach that walked through the city, that the city was rather an incongruent desert, full of people and things—and overwhelming in its solitude. He felt weary, exhausted, as if pressure were falling from the cosmos on his shoulders, pushing him down, threatening to crush him. *Like a cockroach*, he thought.

As if moved by an alien force, he got up, walked to the wall, and raised his hand. The cockroach, perhaps sensing its imminent demise, stopped—the way fear stops us when it is sudden. There they were both, paralyzed. For some inexplicable reason, he thought of his mother. He thought that she must have been just as defenseless when his father came upon her with the machete.

Outside, the world was still a cauldron. The old AC unit in the room at least kept him from sweating. He had been thinking it through for a couple of days and had already decided that, yes, going out looking for a job would be easier than selling drugs. He had tried to contact each one of the selling spots but to no avail. The last time he tried, they didn't even let him speak: a stout guy took out a .38 and put it to his head.

He also went to the barbershops the Deli guy had mentioned before, but felt stupid when they asked him if he had experience cutting hair. They asked him then what experience he had, but kept waiting for his answer. Must still be. Roberto realized at that moment that in his entire life he had learned to do absolutely nothing. His only job had been to stand in the doorway of a bar to bully drunks.

He came out of there with an even heavier load of frustration. Anger was like a fire that scalded his body from his feet to the crown of his skull.

He had not gone three blocks when he saw a sign in a small supermarket. It read: Now hiring man for Deli / Se solicita hombre para Deli.

He hesitated only for a second. After ten minutes of waiting, the manager finally approached him (Roberto let out a sigh of relief when he saw the man was Dominican), asked him a couple of questions, and told him to come back the next day at 7:00 a.m.

Roberto worked in that supermarket for more than three years and, if it hadn't been for the devil who, as the saying goes, is never asleep, his life might have been straightened out at that place. But some people seem to have been born to attract evil to themselves.

The devil, in this case, responded to the name of Shanikwa. She spoke no Spanish but walked as if she wanted to break the walls at her sides with her hips. She had so many curves in that body of hers she could start a business out of it; she knew with great cunning when to bend down, when to neglect the posture of her legs in sit-ups, and when to call for help with the face of a girl about to lose her innocence.

Shanikwa had been there for only a couple of weeks, worked in the butcher's area. Roberto noticed her flirtation from the first moment but, because of their cultural differences (although after three years there, he already spoke the language), he didn't dare to say anything. He also noticed how his co-workers' eyes went after her. "Yo! Dat bitch is fire!" Greg, a good-natured Jamaican dude, said with a smirk.

On a Wednesday, they were scheduled to start in the same shift. Only Roberto, Shanikwa, Elba, and Tomás, the morning supervisor.

Roberto, right knee on the floor, was organizing some boxes when Shanikwa came up behind him and bumped him with her hips. He looked at her. She was smiling. And she just stood there, a narrow foot away, so that if Roberto stood up, their bodies would find themselves inevitably rubbing one against the other.

Evil incarnate leaned forward and whispered something in his ear that Roberto did not really hear. The language of her eyes was unmistakable, though. Roberto got up and, without wasting any more time, grabbed her ass, drew her to him, and kissed her with a combination of fear and fury. Shanikwa reciprocated with the characteristic savagery of one who has longed for and waited too long.

Elba's voice scared them apart. Shanikwa moved away and he, breathless, turned to the boxes, not before seeing her disappear down the hall, the feeling of strong consistency of her ass still in his hands.

They met like this several times in the next three or four days: speechless, in a hurry.

Whenever she could, she would walk past him and grab his cock, or push him to a corner and kiss him, then walk off with a flirtatious, amused giggle. Roberto felt more and more attracted to her: by the whiteness of her mischievous smile, by her voluptuousness, by her daring...

That Monday, it was their turn in the closing shift. Roberto had just set up his register to close the day when Shanikwa arrived and pushed him against the wall. She went over to him with those lips on fire and trapped him with her tongue and its poisonous syrup. This time around, they were going full throttle. She was wearing a little green dress that her left hand slid up while her right one unzipped Roberto's jeans—whose heart beat like a four-hundred-horsepower engine. He grabbed her ass mightily, lifted her to his groin, and right then and there, on top of the counter by the bread and the cheese, they engaged in the delicious battle of sex. He had to cover her mouth with one hand to prevent her moans from being heard.

This, Roberto thought, ecstatic, *is one of those dreams that only happen to other people.*

In a few minutes, when Roberto was about to ejaculate, Shanikwa pulled away, expertly grabbed his dick, and finished the act with her hand. The semen fell on Roberto's pants and she laughed. Putting on a good girl's face, innocent giggle and all, she motioned for him to hurry to the bathroom, to clean up the mess.

When he returned, she was gone. She'd left him a note that read: see ya, luv!

Roberto smiled, finished organizing his work area, took the envelope with the money, deposited it in the safe, and, after a few words with the supervisor, went home.

On his way to the apartment, he thought of Shanikwa. A strange feeling found its way between his lungs and his heart: a mixture of fear and joy. He thought about Ruth and felt a stab in his chest.

The next day, when he got to the supermarket, Greg looked at him with a worried face; and Elba, who wanted to tell him something, could not, since the owner, as soon as he saw him, summoned him to his office. The owner and the manager went in after him. One of the owner's sons was also waiting in there. They all asked him point-blank, as if rehearsed, "Where's the money, Roberto?"

At that moment, everything was terrifyingly clear to him, like a dark veil falling off his eyes. He once again saw it all in his mind's eye like a movie you watch at a slower pace, trying to take in every single detail: Shanikwa seducing him, fucking him, making him cum on his pants, with her little girl's face sending him to the bathroom, and then the note, making fun of his stupidity: *See ya, luv!*

He had left the envelope with the money on the counter. He didn't notice the weight. He didn't notice that it was badly sealed. He didn't realize he'd been served like a fucking *palomo*.

"What money?" He asked, but his face had said more than his words. The three men looked at each other.

The owner said, "Roberto, I don't know what happened. We have seen the cameras… but I do not know..."

"Where did you hide the money?" The son cut off with a bellicose tone.

Roberto looked at him without hiding his anger. "I don't have no money, and *mira a ve cómo tú me habla a mí, montro*."

"I talk to you any way I want. You'd better say where you put those bills, ma nigga, before the police come..." The young man yelled.

His father put his arm in front of him, trying to calm him down. He said, "hey, let's take it easy. Roberto, we don't want any problems, mijo. Tell me what happened and we don't have to get the police involved in this unnecessarily. Where's the money?" The owner's tone was conciliatory.

Roberto then thought of the security cameras and re-membered the owner's comment. "And the camera? You see there who took the money, right? It wasn't me. I don't know shit of no money."

"Dad, call the police already! This motherfucker wants to play smart with us, fuck it!"

Shanikwa's face occupied his mind like a great curtain, like a huge painting that prevented him from seeing the rest of the world. *See ya, luv! I'm a fucking idiot! That son of a bitch!*

"Roberto, say what you know, boy, three thousand do-llars is a lot of money. They can even deport you for that," the old man told him.

Three thousand dollars, Roberto thought, *that son-of-a-bitch stole three thousand dollars by taking me for a fool and left me in the fucking woods.*

"Yo, you fucking dumb? Speak up! Where is the damn money?!"

Roberto jumped up from the chair and broke the boy's nose and mouth with a punch. The boss tried to defend his boy, but Roberto was too strong for him and easily threw him to the ground. Before running off, he gave the arrogant young man one last kick in the ribs and, in Spanglish, said, "Fuck you, *mamagüevo!*"

CHAPTER 17

FOUR TO ONE
(TWO YEARS BEFORE SHANIKWA)

Roberto was off on Sundays. He had mixed feelings about that. On one hand, everyone at work sort of envied him for it: even though he was one of the newer employees, the rest of the positions in the supermarket did not allow for Sundays off—his did. On the other hand, since he had no friends, he rarely felt like doing things outside his tiny, rented room. And because it was Sunday, whatever errand he had to run had to be postponed for a weekday—and, of course, he hardly had any time then and had to be rushing.

That Sunday, however, he wanted to go outside, walk around the city, and just feel like a regular person. *What does a regular person do on a Sunday?* He asked himself as he showered. His strong, dark body was vibrant and shiny under the falling cool water. His fingers massaged with force through his shampooed hair and he thought about his son, how much taller he was getting, how much smarter. *I hope he's eating well.*

Rubbing his head and shoulders dry with the navy towel, he stood before the night table where he kept the latest photos his wife had sent to Whatsapp—which he liked to have printed from a local store nearby. There they were, smiling. Ruth had not aged a single day. Her eyes reflected still that peace he had experienced only with her. And his *muchacho, gee, he looks just like me at that age.*

In another photo, they are in a park. Daniel is wearing a polo and a baseball cap Roberto sent him just a few weeks before. They fit perfectly. Ruth is standing behind him, so that Roberto could see how tall the boy is getting. Roberto thought Daniel was a little chubby and Ruth a tad too thin. He knew better than to tell her that when they talked on the phone. In the photo, her hair has spread to the left as has the skirt of her long, flowery dress. Although her eyes seemed joyful, her smile was struggling to convey whatever amount of joy is necessary to make a photo perfect. There was something in them, he thought. And Roberto wondered if she had already found someone else. *That's not it, you idiot! She misses you. She misses her son's father. My little boy… they miss me. Just like I miss them. That's all.*

Wearing jeans and Nikes, as well as a Yankees hat and t-shirt, he ran down the stairs and entered the bodega. He ordered coffee and talked to Marlon, the clerk, for about seven minutes. He then walked to the train station, refilled his Metrocard, and waited six minutes for the uptown 4 train to Woodlawn.

As usual, the train was packed. He stood by the doors, holding one of the silver rails. Right next to him, a white man in a light-blue shirt and dotted navy tie read the paper. To his left, a Hispanic lady struggled to maintain her balance with four bags and a backpack. Right across, two teenagers, one black, one white, head-phones on, discussed videogame characters. Sitting to his right, the row of strangers started with a middle-eastern woman in her thirties, then a white grumpy-looking man in his fifties, and then a young woman, black and beautiful, wearing a dark pink t-shirt that read 'PraiseTheLord'. Their eyes met for a brief second. Sitting across from her, two black men dozed off. They looked like they had a rough night at work.

Twenty people in a single wagon. All strangers. All keeping to themselves.

Roberto wondered if his life would have been different there in New York had the circumstances that brought him been different. He nodded. *I probably would have never left the island if… yeah. I don't think I would have left them.*

He wondered how many of these people had also been forced by their circumstances to come over or do things with their lives they would rather not do. How many were commuting to or from a job they did not want because they made the wrong decisions or because of someone else. He glanced at several of them and thought he saw a similarity in their eyes. This lasted but a second, surely, and it probably meant nothing.

We're all just sad and lonely here, aren't we?

When the train reached Fordham Road, he stepped out. This was where he came whenever he had to buy clothes or sneakers. It was a wide and long street, lined with stores of all sizes and variety, and cramped with Dominicans and blacks.

At his favorite Pizza place, he ordered a slice of pizza and a coke, and chewed slowly as he observed the bustle and hustle of the street. Not in a million years he would have guessed New York would be brimming with street vendors, homeless people, and street scammers of all sorts, just like in *el patio.*

Suddenly, the shadow that always hunted him cast its dark and wide wings over him and the pizza did not taste as good and the street did not seem as inviting. He shook his head and looked down. He tried to force the thoughts out of his mind. It was impossible. He knew he had no power over this hatred. He knew whenever the thought of his father crossed his mind, the world stepped back into the darkness that governed his days and nights.

There were days, sure, when life rolled on so naturally he just thought, well, maybe, just maybe… but those days did not last. This hatred, this primal sense of revenge, this was what moved him forward. This darkness was the engine that kept him going.

Ruth would tell him to stop chasing vengeance, to focus on them, on his family. She would tell him she and his son loved him and the only way they would be back together was if he chose them over that vendetta. The first time she said this, he got so upset, he hung up the phone on her. He did not call her back for the next three days, both out of shame and regret.

But Roberto knew she was right. He knew this path of blood would only keep him away from his family. He also knew his mother's death could not go unpunished.

What is a man without his word? What good is a man if he cannot avenge his own mother? What am I supposed to do? Just forget that mother-fucker butchered her? How the fuck could I ever live happily knowing how he killed her, how he destroyed all possibility of happiness for us?!

This is what he was thinking, the last bite of pizza in his right hand, when he heard the voice of the young black boy, sixteen at the most, ask him where some particular sneakers store was.

Though his English had improved, he still had difficulties understanding people with accents and those who spoke really fast. So, out of habit, he always asked people to repeat themselves for confirmation.

Sorry? What? Sneakers?

And then he saw it. On this kid's face. He saw his attention had been diverted. He saw the malice, the trick. He understood he had been played.

Shit!

That first punch, Roberto thought he was dead. He felt the blow, the pain, and the disconnection from reality all at the same time. The darkness he had experienced moments before gave way to a different kind of absolute obscurity, of a sort he had never known: the darkness of unconsciousness. Several minutes later, he would come to understand that this darkness was, as a matter of fact, a type of mercy from the mysteries of life: it prevented him from feeling the following two minutes of kicks and punches the four black teenagers showered him with.

When he came to, his sneakers, his hat, and his dignity were gone. He was left on the floor, a bloody pulp, and all he heard was a woman's voice, clearly Dominican, that said: "Look, this Dominican piece of shit! That's what all these assholes come here for, to sell drugs and damage our good names."

CHAPTER 18

THE WORD 'ARRIMAO'

Some words denigrate. Some words dismember a man's dignity. They affect some people more than they do others. A matter of pride, of upbringing. The word *arrimao* always affected me. It's always been a terrible word, a seven-letter slap. It was the one thing even the poorest people found disgust for back in the hood. It means you're of no use. You're living in someone else's house as a burden to them. It means you're free-loading, sucking off someone else's life. It doesn't matter if this someone is family or a close friend, if they treat you well or not, living in their house means you're always an obstacle, dead-weight that they have to carry about or maneuver around until who-knows-when-or-what.

This was the one word I'd always feared. Even later on, after I'd gotten a steady job and was dutifully paying rent and helping out at my aunt's, it was impossible to avoid this feeling, this sinking sensation that I'd been the dead beat in the rhythm of this already shattered family. It did not matter if, like Dulce used to say to ease my soul, everyone who comes to New York has to go through the process of being arrimao for a week or two, a month or six, a full damn year; it didn't matter if she repeated tirelessly that I wasn't arrimao in her house but a welcome addi-tion to her family and her peace of mind. None of it mattered because, true or not, I did get to live in her house for months as lice live in heads: sucking people's blood irresponsibly. Being arrimao inevitably left me feeling like I was nothing but a loser.

So, when Dulce told me that we had to move because the owners of the apartment were requesting it, it felt like I was striding to the wall before the firing squad.

There I was without a job, without documents, without money, and about to be thrown out to the street like a dirty rag. Dulce began to cry. The future was uncertain for them, too. I tried to comfort her but there were no words. We both stood in granite silence, a wall of silence that rose gigantic. The word arrimao and the word uncertainty walk together. I was mad at myself because I was being selfish: I was worried about my future when these two kids and this woman would probably end up on the street, in a shelter, one of those shitty places where homeless people queue endlessly to be able to spend the night. *They probably won't even let me enter a shelter without papers,* I thought sadly.

Three days later, having just woken up, Dulce knocked on the bedroom door for me to come to the phone. "It's Tatica, your aunt," she said. It was nice talking to Aunt Tatica. I hadn't heard from her in a long time. We talked for a long while: about Abu, about the situation in Santo Domingo, about mom and the sweets (Oh, your mother, ironing and washing and selling sweets, damn it!), about my friend Pope and his awning business, about Julio Gallina who kept counting some imaginary numbers of something that nobody ever understood, about el Espaldú who was still in the same job and had already bought his house...

As we spoke, it seemed as if I had left el patio forty years before, like they were all strangers whom I had seen once or twice in another lifetime. I wanted to lie to her when she asked me how I was doing, but the truth came out of my mouth like the stone that killed Goliath. "Easy, boy," aunt Tatica said, "let me make a few calls and I'll take care of that for you, you calm down."

She hung up and left me entertaining a tiny hope. I waited for her call all day. Around eight o'clock in the evening, I settled down in my room and cried helplessly. Then I berated myself for crying like a cupcake.

She called the next day at the same time. "Go to 2816 36th Street, that's your Aunt Carla's house. I've already talked to her and she's delighted that you're going to live with her, to keep her company," she told me.

I didn't know much about Aunt Carla. She was one of those cousins of someone in the family who, because she was older, was already your aunt. I did remember seeing her a couple of times. I knew she got along with Mom and that, like everyone else, she adored Abu.

"Gather your things and off you go, she's wait-ing for you. I send you a hug, dear, and take it easy."

I felt myself levitate with relief. That same af-ternoon I spoke with Dulce. It was hard. I felt that, somehow, I was be-traying them by accepting my aunt's proposal. *You are the lousy captain of the sinking ship. Running away at the first trickle of water,* my conscience told me. But there was no meanness in this woman. She wished me luck and told me not to worry, that everyone had to do what they could to survive. We nodded at the same time and then she stood up, grabbed the old coffee maker, and readied the coffee.

One of her boys was jumping from one piece of fur-niture to another while the other one tried to read a comic book. "*Mira, muchacho de la mierda,* I'm going to take your liver out with

a spoon and leave it right there for you to put it back yourself." I
had to laugh at such a crazy threat.

*****

Aunt Carla was a sweetheart but her house was a pigsty.
It had a single bedroom, a small living room (where we improvised an air mattress for me), a tiny bathroom, and a kitchen the
size the living room should have been. It had a little garden at the
entrance that looked like a Don King sculpture made of grass;
and everything, everything, absolutely everything seemed dirty
from centuries, as if the knowledge of water and detergent had
never come around. Aunt Carla didn't seem to notice any of this.
The power of habit, I thought, *exactly how it goes with marriages*. I
thought of Marielita.

"Mijo, make yourself comfortable. Over there, yes, you
can put your clothes in that *armarito*... no, don't worry, I don't use
it, I don't have anything, I'm old now... be careful with the
cockroaches..."

Aunt Carla walked with more patience than balance. Her
little elf body and brown flip-flops made me think of *Hoy no quiero
cantar,* that sad and beautiful song by Leo Favio my sister and I
used to love and sing so much.
She asked me if I was hungry and set out to cook something that almost immediately smelled like glory. I fell asleep on
the stained tablecloth and she woke me up by rubbing my head
with one hand while arranging the spoon and knife with the

other. Her gesture evoked my mother's hands as she patted me when either anger or disillusion took a hold of me.

There, with Aunt Carla, I spent the poorest six months of my life. But there, also, I learned that poverty and humility are two different things. Although not all the poor are humble and not all the humble are poor, there is nothing like the most acid misery to learn to value the truly important things in life. Living with so little made me think of Abu all the more often. Sometimes it seemed that I could hear his tired voice telling me there was nothing in New York.

When I saw the very first snowfall, I spent hours staring out the window. The snow seemed like magic to me: the whitish wind, the distance melted into a whiteness that made me want to jump on it. There was something majestic yet mysterious about the clarity of it, something melancholy about the way the snow-flakes fell, slowly at first then whirling, then in flurries. And then there was some soothing quality I'd never before experienced with anything, not even with the tranquil rain on the tin roof back in my street, la Baltasara.

I saw the train go by quickly, the people in their coats, so big on them it got hard to walk. I saw men and women with shovels trying to free their cars from the embrace of the early morning precipitation. The top of cars, how the snow seemed like gray-white wigs on them. And then surely I saw the faces of Mariel and my Mom's in the shy reflection of the window glass. It was as if their memories came out of my head and projected themselves on the window.

On more than one occasion, Aunt Carla found me with my face in the crook of my arm, crying softly. Sometimes she'd leave me alone. Other times, she'd say, "easy, boy, everything will work out fine in the end. You'll see."

When spring came, Aunt Carla began her annual bout of pollen allergies. I didn't know what that was. There's no such thing as pollen allergies in DR, or dust allergies, or bug-bite allergies… the poor tropical people cannot afford such fancy illnesses. So, it was hard, and weird, for me to see how every day she got worse, with tears, asthma attacks, sneezing... She acted normal as if it weren't evident that Death had her scythe pointed at her.

One morning, I woke up and she wasn't home. I was so worried that I called the only son she had, Miguelo.

"I took her to the clinic earlier. She got really sick," he told me, not a hint of recrimination, not a hint of concern.

"But why didn't you wake me up?" I asked him, more sternly than I would have liked. "I don't know," he said dryly, then apologized; said they were calling him, and hung up.

After a while, he called me to say aunt was not doing well and would probably have to stay with them for a while. "And the house?" I asked and immediately regretted it. I didn't want him to think I was imposing. "I don't know, stay there. Aren't you working yet?" He asked me. I said I wasn't and he told me he'd ask around in the marketplace. Called me two days later, gave me an address, and told me to ask for Don Tico.

Don Tico hired me right away. It was a produce business located in a place called Hunts Point, famous for selling fruit. I got up at 3:30 a.m. every day and spent ten hours activating boxes, cleaning warehouses, peeling watermelons, traveling in trucks around the city, watering and delivering produce everywhere... the truth is that even though I arrived with cracked hands, sore arms, and dog-tiredness, every Friday evening I came home with an ear-to-ear smile on my face: I had never made so much money in my entire life. New York was starting to look just a little bit like what I'd expected.

My first true joy in this country was the day I was able to send money to Abu, Mariel, and my Mom. That morning, on my way to Western Union, I remembered Dulce's voice, *The American Dream.*

*****

When Miguelo called the marqueta, when they told me he was calling, I knew before I heard his voice that Aunt Carla had passed away.

A week before, I had visited her. We talked about work, the weather, the Yankees and the Mets... It seemed to me that she had lost weight, that her eyelids were so heavy they tilted her all the way forward. When I was at the door that day, ready to leave, I told Miguelo my impressions. "Yeah, she's really old, ain't she," was all he said.

Fewer than fifteen people attended Aunt Carla's wake. Seven of those were members of her congregation at church, two were relatives neither I nor her son had ever met, and the others were there probably for the free coffee and crackers.

I remember her lying in that cramped wooden space. Illogically, I hoped she was comfortable. Despite the cruelty of death, I found that she still didn't seem trapped in the corrupting hideousness of it. She seemed rather… liberated—as if freed from the ongoing burdens of monotony, stupid allergies, and the choice of caring for other people's sadness.

This uncalled-for thought came to mind then, *por un beso que te dé, nada en el mundo importará, y en un instante entenderás completamente, que tu alma es mía para siempre y siempre…* lyrics to a Salsa song about death, telling how it was always lurking and inevitable, and, in the end, poetic.

I remember sitting down, sipping my coffee, when the vision of my own funeral came to me. *How many people will attend?* All of a sudden, I felt like I was drowning. Short of breath. I was possessed by the already familiar urge to cry. Yet this time it was more like a slap. I put both hands to my face and gave vent to my tears. Those present surely believed I was crying for that aunt whom I had only known for months. And a part of me was, a part of me cried for that kind-hearted old woman who took me in and made me *pastelitos* and let me be another lonely *arrimao* in her living room. But the truth is that, for the most part, I was crying because of the fragility of being alive, because of the constant decision-making that leads to failure and loneliness, because of the obvious ill-will of people… I felt fear, fear of living my whole life without consequence, of going through the paths of life and not sowing anything, not contributing anything, not leaving a mark. Not even the certainty of having loved correctly or having given everything to those who deserved it.

And that made me recall something else, verses from Dante's Inferno, which, for once, brought me no joy:

"...for he who rests on down or under covers cannot come to fame, and he who spends his life without renown leaves such a vestige of himself on earth as smoke bequeaths to air or foam to water."

A week later, Miguelo phoned to say the house had to be handed over. I tried to ask him if something could be done for me to keep the responsibility, but he wouldn't listen.

I never understood Miguelo. He was a savage beast that someone or something had just managed to tame well enough not to go rampant murdering people around—if such a thing can be imagined.

From his customary indifference, he cruised to the most ridiculous bad mood in a matter of just a few days. He called in a threatening tone, even said that my staying in that house was like making fun of his mother's memory.

At one point, I wanted to believe that this change responded to the pain of loss, that the poor man did not know how to cope with his feelings. But, truth be told, I think Miguelo was just a strange soul, a seemingly insufferable, inexcusable man.

*****

The first night, I stared at the ceiling, at the walls with the hanging diplomas and medals, the desk full of papers, envelopes, receipts, pencils, folders... and let out a sigh.

Don Tico had given me permission to stay in his office, "as long as you need to, *chamaco*." He'd said.

Beggars, or arrimaos, can't be choosers, I thought drily. There was that word again, like the chorus of the song that you hate, yet, against your will, always comes back to your head: closer, closer.

I walked slowly in circles inside the narrow office. A thousand thoughts in my head. A thousand feelings. I touched the backs of the chairs. I touched the wood of the desk, a painting of Saint Michael with his fiery sword threatening *al pájaro malo*, a shelf with half a dozen books. My eyes fell on an old, chocolate-colored tome. I read out loud, "The Power and the Glory." I did not remember who, but someone had recommended it to me once.

Don Tico had an inflatable bed and a good heater. He would reassure me whenever he got a chance, "Stay put, *chamaco*, you're not a problem to me."

He was a good man, Don Tico. His untimely death hurt me deeply. Damn cancer. Ate him very quickly, or maybe it was that stubbornness of ours to ignore the body and its signs. The truth is that one day we found out he was sick and in four months he was gone. I'll always be grateful to him for hiring me, but even more so for the three weeks he put up with me in that office.

When I finally found a room to rent, it was in an apartment of a guy people called Durán, one of my co-workers. (I never knew if Durán was his first name, last name, or if anyone had seen in him a resemblance to the Panamanian legend, boxer *Manos de Piedra*. I surely didn't.) He lived with his wife, Onelia, and their son, Luis, who had Down syndrome.

Even when I saw little of them, even paying for that room religiously, I couldn't help feeling I was still *arrimao* in that house, that my presence there interrupted the logic of their home.

Unlike Dulce, this woman was quiet and lonely. Most of the time, I would see her sit on the ledge of the window and gaze out at the world with a cup of coffee in her hand, just chilling there, absentminded. She'd spend hours like that, idle in that position: sitting uncomfortably, watching the bustle of others, thinking about God-only-knows-what.

The only time we spoke to each other was when I handed her the rent money. I would ask her about the child and she'd always say he was doing well, improving in school. Then she would excuse herself and go to the kitchen and I would go back to my room, to watch television or to read some of the books that I bought from a man across the street.

One Saturday, late into the night, I was awakened by an uproar. Durán and his wife were fighting. Durán had a mistress. When the argument boiled up, I wanted to step out of the room and try to reason with them, but reason itself stopped me: I could not get involved in these matters because I was not friends with these people.

From one moment to the next, the screaming stopped and then I heard the front door open and close with violence.

As I left my room the next morning, Onelia was sitting in her usual place on the window edge, looking out at the world. I said good morning through my teeth and proceeded to pour myself a cup of coffee. (It was the only thing we had learned to share in that house; the only gesture of trust that had been given me or I'd been willing to take.)

Without looking at me, she replied, "Good morning," and, to my surprise, added, "there is no sugar left in the can. Take it from down there, from a big box in there somewhere."

I knew that had been the longest sentence I had ever heard her utter. In silence, I did what she told me while trying to guess what things were going through her mind. I don't know if it was the fact that Durán hadn't spent the night at the house or why the hell, but, for the first time that morning, I felt she was, after all, an attractive woman.

Like that, with her back to me, her body looked slender despite the robe and pajama bottoms. She had long dark hair, and her complexion was the color of coffee when you pour a lot of milk in it. She had bony hands, short nails, and sad eyes.

I think she realized I was staring at her. She turned her face and looked me in the eye. "Anything the matter?" She asked. Her voice, her tone, revealed nothing. "No, nothing," I replied softly, my gaze fleeing from hers. She looked back at the street.

Just as I was about to go back to the room, she told me, "Durán is not going to return to this house. Now it will be just the three of us." Her voice was firm, without hesitation, the voice of the foreman issuing an order. As if what she had said required clarification, she added, "just the child, you, and me."

An hour later, getting dressed for mass (my mother had made me promise I'd go even if just once a month), a mundane philosophy occupied me: Why right at the moment of attraction I'm always turned on by the things that are the least sexual: hair on the shoulders, a bare forearm, the gesture of moving a shred of hair behind an ear, a grimace that hints at a smile, the sweet resonance of laughter? I thought of Onelia. "Drop it," I protested out loud.

When I went in the living room, I saw her picking up things that little Luis had thrown on the floor. She was wearing loose jeans and a Boston Celtics t-shirt. When she heard the door, she glanced sideways. "Are you coming to eat? I'm cooking," she asked as she picked up a piece of a cardboard puzzle from behind the sofa. "Oh, yeah... Okay, I'm coming," I replied, babbling like an idiot. She said O.K. without looking at me, stood up, and moved on to the kitchen.

When I entered this house of the Lord, I felt a slight disappointment. I don't know why I had expected this church to impress me. It was, however, just like any other church I had ever visited. The Christ on the cross bled lightly from his wounds, his face bore the same expression of sadness that had always seemed incongruous to me—I expected to find a suffering Christ, whose face spoke of pain, not sorrow. The paintings of the procession were the same, too, as well as the statue of the Virgin with the baby Jesus in her arms. The boy had always seemed an aberration to me: Why was he white and cherub-like?

The priest came in with his long white cassock and gold decorations. The altar boys carried cymbals and other things I could not make out. The music resounded in every inch of that place as if trying to reach heaven itself. The parishioners, most of them well-dressed, entered silently, crossed themselves, and greeted their acquaintances by gesturing with their hands. They all smiled.

By the corners, some older people were getting ready to later collect the tithe. What I did like about this mass was the Father. He was a kind-looking man not yet in his sixties. He was chubby and short, and his hands gestured with the grace and rhythm of an orchestra director. During the homily, he spoke of values in modern society, of the right way of raising children, of never stopping talking to them and explaining good from evil.

"What happens, mom and dad, is that, if we do not educate them now, if we don't teach them now the value of what we give them, if we don't let them know about the sacrifices we make to educate them, to feed them, to buy their clothes and their toys… tomorrow they will grow up believing that these things cost us nothing; tomorrow, when it is their turn to be parents, they will not have the foundation to educate their own children. That is the chain of ignorance and lack of values that we must avoid..."

One time, we had been to church: Mariel, her mother, and I. Mariel wore a beautiful white dress with burgundy little flowers. We sat close to the pulpit. The Father, taking her little hand, gave her his blessing. He was a very humble and friendly man, that Father. He did not speak with bombast and was always ready to listen to everyone.

That day, once mass was over and we were all standing outside the church saying our good-byes, he asked me how things were going at home. "Going," I answered, unable to lie to him. He put his hand on my shoulder and, smiling with a mixture of understanding and support, said, "I'm here for you if you ever want to talk."

Mariel ran out at that moment and I had to go catch up with her. I had words stuck in my throat. I would have liked to talk a little more with him, but other people had already approached him. I waved goodbye. I think we both knew in some mysterious way that this inconclusive conversation already foresaw, somehow, the inevitability of the collapse of my home.

Back at the church in the Bronx, I was well aware of the moment when everyone stands to hug and to wish *la paz*. So, I got up and went out right before. I surprised myself walking fast—I always walk like a snail to a slaughterhouse.

It was hot at the end of the morning and the sweat in my armpits bothered me. When I got on the bus, I thought of Onelia sitting at her window, sipping her coffee in silence, and watching life go by like someone watching a boring program on TV. When I came to realize it, it was too late: I had a notorious lump that threatened to unzip my pants.

CHAPTER 19

A FATAL MISTAKE

The shots sounded like bombs. With each explosion, a startle.

"Over here, over here," Ricardo shouted nervously. They followed him. Roberto was last, watching from the corner, shielded by the wall. That door led to another narrow corridor where there was a metal staircase so tall, they thought it led all the way to heaven. Roberto and Ricardo looked at each other. Then nodded. They had no way to know this was the way to reach the adjacent building, the warehouse that the owner of both buildings had co-joined for his convenience.

"Come on, let's go up, run," Ricardo told them. Roberto didn't say a word, it was almost as if Ricardo had been promoted to commander-in-chief of their escape. As they climbed, they heard the policemen as they got closer. It seemed stupid to Roberto to be going last but there was nothing he could do then. The stair-case was too narrow to slip through.

"Move, move, you, cunts, or I'll knock you down, move," he yelled at the women.

Ricardo thought Roberto's voice sounded different, unconvinced. He looked at him askance. He was exhausted, yes, but it wasn't just that. It seemed to him that Roberto had finally realized the crossroads he was at. Everything had turned crystal clear now: he would not get out of this alive. It was perhaps the unaccepted resignation of he who knows himself trapped what Ricardo heard in Roberto's voice. The awareness that everything he had done had inexorably led him to this point that, in his bizarre planning of the robbery, he'd quite never envisioned.

Before ending his next threat to the women, Roberto felt a hot bite on his left thigh. Almost at the same time, he heard the roar of the shot. "Coño!" he screamed. Right away, he fired three rounds of his own. But the policemen had taken cover.

"Move your fucking asses, damn it! these fucking faggots shot me!" Roberto yelled with a child's voice.

Two more policemen arrived, shot at him several times but missed. In a matter of minutes, they were all gone from sight, out of the cops' range.

"Keep going this way, this way... there's gotta be another room on the other side, come on," Ricardo told them. When he looked back, Roberto was sitting on the floor holding his legs. "I can't run no more," he said, panting.

The women hesitated for just an instant. They glimpsed at one another and started running down the long corridor that promised an exit. Fearing that Roberto would shoot them, Ricardo called them to stop, but they ignored him. They were going like crazy, running side by side, as if in a race.

Roberto watched them run away. A part of him wanted to raise the gun. Instead, he just stared at them—they looked like two dolls running awkwardly.

When they finally reached the door, a window-pane exploded in uncountable shards and the brunette's head snapped back. It was the same movement as John F. Kennedy's head in the black-and-white clip when the bullet hits him and no one knows what's happened.

The blonde's scream was creepy. As creepy as the cold, dense silence that engulfed both Roberto and Ricardo.

CHAPTER 20

COUSIN MONCHI

Monchi, his cousin, picked him up from a *bodega*. As they drove, Roberto told him all the details about the mess with Shanikwa and the people from the supermarket.

"Yo, that bitch! You can't trust no woman, bro!" Monchi complained. "But nah, ma nigga, easy; I got'cha here."

The little town was full of one- and two-story houses, mostly painted pastel colors, with wooden or iron gates. There were small gardens in the front, big backyards, and only a handful of people who walked their dogs on the sidewalks.

At first, Roberto didn't know how to discern the differrence he perceived in the air, in the environment, beyond the appearance of the place or the number of people and vehicles.

It was later, after a couple of weeks had passed, that he realized it: the overwhelming stillness of the place stunned him.

It took them about an hour to get to their destination. The sunset was quite like nothing he had witnessed before.

"...I don't hustle here, nigga, my shit's over in Boston. About forty minutes north. That's where the magic happens, ya feel me? Here, I do my little pretend job in an auto shop and I do fine, but on the weekends, *loco*, I go down there and make the real coin."

Monchi was smoking a cigarette as he spoke. Roberto had a cold beer in his right hand, a blunt in the left. They were now on the porch of the little nice house Monchi rented.

The night was visited by a cool breeze that every now and then threatened to grow colder. "Bro, I gotta find something to do. The money I saved, I'm going to eat it all if I don't find some gig soon." Roberto said, almost in a whisper. He took a good look around and commented, "and over here, bro, all these *come mierda* look at you like you're a rabid dog." He didn't know that for sure, but somehow felt it was true.

Roberto attempted a sip as he thought that the place couldn't be as bad as New York, but there was nothing left in the bottle. He put it on the edge of the railing and gave the blunt a tug.

"Take me to Boston, loco, I'll hustle," he said. "Yo, you crazy, bro. This ain't like back in DR; I bring some nigga *pal bloque*, they kill me."

Roberto looked at his cousin (his impotence the size of the sky that had already allowed a handful of stars to show their timid lights), and asked, "and what the fuck am I gonna do here, *manin?*"

Monchi nodded in understanding. After a few seconds, he said, "You just take it easy, *loco*. We'll figure it out. *No te ponga bruto, manin*, you'll see how everything will be just fine in the end."

That weekend, Monchi took him to the auto shop and got him a job washing parts and cars. "Ain't much, bro, but it's better than nothing, iight?" Monchi told him when he got in the car.

Once home, they shook hands and Monchi pulled away, leaving him on the sidewalk. Across the street, walking at a slow pace, a woman in her early sixties walked a dog bigger than she was. When she saw Roberto, she tugged on the collar chain and quickened her pace. Didn't even bother to hide it.

Two months later, on a cold Tuesday night, a truck pulled up in front of the house and a voice Roberto had never heard before called his name. Cautiously, he looked outside through one of the windows. He saw two guys carrying Monchi, who had bandages all over and looked like shit.

"Fuck! What happened?!" he asked as he ran to them.

"He got shot, bro, down in B, better get inside and watch out. You know a doctor, call'im asap. Manin ain't well," said one of the two guys in their early twenties. That said, they drove away.

Roberto looked at Monchi's face and just could not believe this was happening. Just as he had feared.

"They shot... me in Boston... *loco*..." he said with evident difficulty. Roberto told him to shut up. "I'm alive ... don't know... how," Monchi stuttered.

A similar scene had played in Roberto's unresting mind for days. Monchi never spent longer than the weekend in Boston, but this time it had already been over a week. He had tried his cell phone but it had been going straight to voice mail.

"Damn, *loco, coño*, who did this shit, bro? Tell me they caught'em!"
"No, no... forget about that... best... nobody... knows... the monkeys... they'll want to investigate and shit... no good for me... better... leave shit like this, bro." Monchi coughed and grunted in pain.

Roberto helped him up to his room, accommodated him as best he could. Two hours later, Monchi was sleeping and Roberto wondered what the hell was going to happen. What he earned didn't even cover a quarter of the rent. The agreement with Monchi had been that he would live there on the condition of taking care of the house—and of the merchandise he kept in secret places.
Monchi took care of the expenses. All Roberto bought was his own food. *Shit!* Inhaling deeply, Roberto thought, *what the fuck am I gonna do? There is no fucking way I can make rent.*

Every time things got complicated for him, his father's face showed up in his mind like the specter of a dead child wandering around a large deserted house. Anger clouded his thoughts. All of his problems were that damn man's fault. All of them. Sometimes he wanted to slash open his arms, his legs, watch the blood run until he could no longer see it. It wasn't suicide he was after: it was the disgust of knowing that his blood was the same blood that ran through that motherfucker's cursed veins. He wanted to get rid of that wretched blood—get rid of all ties to that man, responsible for all his misery and bitterness.

He put both hands to his face. Seeing his father's face brought with him the other visions: the machete, the broken voice of the professor who gave him the news, the face of his dead mother, a pool of blood that he never actually saw but was somehow imprinted in his mind...

They spent the first snow of the year in the hospital. Despite Monchi's pleas and weak tantrums, Roberto had to take him to the hospital because he was getting worse by the day. One of the wounds had gotten infected and they didn't realize it until it was late. Since then, they'd had to make emergency trips to the clinic far too often. And even there, Monchi had been battling for his life for the past two months already. Roberto knew the doctors and nurses were aware that these were firearm wounds. He didn't know how or why no one had called the police on them already.

Roberto, on the other hand, was desperate. They owed three months of rent. The eviction notices had started to arrive and Roberto had had two unpleasant encounters with the landlord—a tall white man no younger than seventy who carried a gun in his waistband. *Like this the fucking wild west.*

What he earned was barely enough to eat. He had tried to take over Monchi's business in Boston but got blocked.

"They turned... on us... loco," Monchi said, his voice broken, like his body and his soul.

Watching the snow, how it had been falling at the same quiet pace as the hours of that night, Roberto thought of his wife and son. Although he saw them often through social media and video calls, their faces in his memory were for some reason the faces they had when he left them, when his son was but a cute little thing and his wife still had a trace of hope in her smile. He wondered, as all men who travel off do, how things might have been different had he stayed. He wondered, seeing his dying cousin on that bed, and himself, so alone and so damn broke, whether or not all this misery could have been avoided just by looking into his wife's eyes that day Nilo went to get him and seeing her pleas in her brown irises.

His own eyes threatened a tear or two, and, man as he was, he acted like something had gotten in them and wiped them off. There was no one else in that room besides silent broken Monchi and, still, he felt the need to act tough, to never break character. *You're a fucking actor,* he lectured himself in his mind, *been acting tough your whole fucking life but you're just a damn coward, un maldito pendejo is what you are.*

He then looked somewhere beyond the snow. What was this which he sensed out there in the vastness of the great darkness? Something was waiting for him. Something he did not know. At that moment, he felt an inexplicable connection with that mysterious somethingness and his eyes filled with tears. He wept in silence for a few minutes and felt the embrace of relief as he allowed his soul this liberating occurrence. Never before had he experienced anything of the sort. Never before had he allowed himself a second of vulnerability. He just sat there. Quiet. Weeping. And then, when he felt curiously light and surrounded by a warm sensation (that he would have called peace), he looked up again. He was trying to figure out what this was. This thing, almost mystical, that he sensed was looking back at him from a distance.

He then closed his eyes and, in no time, drifted away.

CHAPTER 21

LOVE THAT WAS AND THEN WAS NOT

When Onelia opened the door, I was awakened by the common scent of clean things, the dim light from the hallway, and the vague alarm of those who sense the violation of their personal space.

I saw her and kept quiet—as quiet as the tension of such a moment permits. She groped towards me. In the dimness, she resembled a thin naked thief— crawling onto my bed and tripping over my calves and my waist. Though impossible, it seemed to me that I could hear the pounding of her heart. Mine, I felt, was deftly trying to imitate the rhythm of hers.

She brought her mouth to my mouth and, before slithering her tongue in, caught my cock tightly in her right hand—as if afraid it would escape…

Every single time, after making love, I wanted to ask her to stay. Sometimes I grabbed her hand, stroked her hair, her neck... She allowed it, briefly, and then she'd stand, without a word, walk to the door, and let herself be swallowed by the dim light of the hallway.

Every now and then, Durán, drunk, knocked on the apartment door. First, he would insult her, and then he would beg. I felt sorry for him more than once. And more than once, too, I felt ashamed of being there with that indecipherable woman, of listening to that man cry, of knowing that there was a child with mental problems in that household.

One time, some part of me, the macho part surely, wanted to walk out to him and tell him that she was mine now, that he ought to have some self-pride, some dignity and stop chasing after her like a stranded little dog. But another part of me, the part of whatever conscience I had left, advised, instead, *Stay out of it.*

Although I refused to admit it at first, I had fallen in love with this strange woman. I had fallen in love with her silences, her loneliness, her smell of freshly-washed clothes, her bony body, and her still young and firm skin. In that strange ritual, in that extraordinary relationship of pure sexual and clandestine reciprocity, we spent four long years. Onelia never asked for nor accepted anything from me. My nocturnal company was, without the need to articulate it, all she ever wanted.

Many times, I wondered if she loved me; if, perhaps, like me, she had fallen in love and did not dare to face it for fear of the usual complications. Every night, after she left my room, I wondered if, had we dared to say something, maybe we would have found a way, perhaps not to happiness, but at least to the courage we needed to face love.

Our end came with the same irrationality and surprise as our beginning. I waited for her that night, awake, anxious. I fell asleep but never knew what time sleep overcame me. The next day, we said good morning and drank coffee in silence, as always, as if nothing had changed, as if we had made love the night before or as if it was not strange that we had not.

Onelia concentrated on the passers-by. I, on maintaining my willpower not to talk to her about us. Since that morning, she never went back to my room.

Two months later, Durán returned home with a back-pack and two plastic bags. He looked battered, disheveled, but happy.

I wanted to go to my room the second I saw him at the threshold to avoid the hypocrisy of greetings and welcomes, but he gave me no time. He hugged me as if we had at one time been friends and asked how I was doing. I hadn't seen him since he'd left the house. He had even quit his job.

For five or ten minutes, he spoke about every possible thing he could think of. It was as if all this time he'd spent out there had changed him, turned him into an even lamer version of himself. During his time before the break-up, I never heard him speak three sentences in a row.

At one point, Onelia and I finally looked at each other. There was nothing on her face. Durán had returned and that was that.

After a month, I moved out. I left them the way ungrateful people do: without notice or even saying good-bye.

*****

The apartment was small. The single room took up most of the space. It had a tiny kitchen and a hallway that led to the bathroom—where the toilet and a rusty tub fitted well enough for my legs not to bump against anything. The owner had been careful also, thoughtful I would say, with the stove and the refrigerator. She had even left a most comfortable sofa.

I remember that apartment fondly. It was my first one—the one that took me off the list of the arrimao. The 4 and 2 trains were close by. It took only thirty minutes to get to my job. Nine hundred odd days, I reckon, I spent in that place. I do not know, though, how much loneliness or how many tears I shed there, too. I couldn't tell how many times I wanted to leave my dreams behind, grab whatever money I had saved, and take the first plane to my homeland.

So many things happened during my stay in that apartment, both good and bad. I remember it was there, washing dishes after dinner, that Mariel called and told me she'd met a boy. She was a teenager already. I knew it would happen, sooner or later. Still, I swallowed what felt like sandpaper and dropped one of the spoons. The silence that took hold of me was the embodiment of a man, a tall, muscular man, who held me so tight I felt my body would break. "*Aló, ¿papi? ¿Tú ta ahí?*" she asked, her voice eerily womanly all of a sudden, her tone concerned.

So many things ran wild through my head at that moment, so much regret, so much impotence. I got irrationally upset and helpless. We held on to the connection for long, odd minutes of dense silence, interrupted only by the sound of my frantic, aimless pacing and Mariel's scared voice asking if I was Okay.

Another evening, it was mami who called. How dreadful for the illegal immigrant to see the name of any beloved person on the cell phone screen at an hour they hardly ever call. An abyss opens wide in one's chest and there's a moment of hesitation. An urge to just let that thing ring eternally so you don't have to know what the terrible news might be. I said, "*sí, mami, ¿Qué pasó?* She said she was fine but her voice betrayed a sorrow. I asked if she was Okay, if Mariel was, and she said yes, they were all fine, but she had sad news: my good friend Yovanny had had a stroke.

I remember a distinct fragility in the way she articulated these words. I sensed how massive this action felt in my mother's heart: telling me one of my closest friends was seriously ill. I felt instant sadness over this terrible news, but also, inexplicably, I felt a strange proximity to her, to her love. A proximity I'd always known existed but which had, up to that moment, remained unstirred, taken for granted. I somehow felt her love manifested in her understanding of how hurtful this news was to me. So powerful, and beautiful, this sensation of closeness with my mother was, that, for a moment, it became a sort of shield, a warm embrace, that soothed and sheltered me, that illuminated and caressed me, that strengthened every fiber of my being. Never before had I wished or needed to hug my mother as deeply as I did then. And, yet, never had I felt her closer.

*****

One afternoon, arriving from the marketplace, a robust-looking guy standing by the corner eyed me up and down. He had light skin and dark hair. His unshaved chin made me think of *el chómpiras*, yet it was obvious this man was not there to make me laugh. I passed by him cautiously. He fired a sudden question, "you live here, pal?" I scowled at him. On the street, you learn

148

not to show fear—even if you're about to shit your pants. "Yeah, why?" The big fellow shook his head and arched down his lips with the slowest motion possible, as if to mean: 'no reason.' I walked up the stairs but never stopped looking back.

That was the first day of the siege. Although we never exchanged words again, for a little less than a month I ran into this character almost every day. Sometimes he was at the door of the building. Others, just nearby or standing by the same corner. Most of the time he was alone. What never changed was the look in his eyes. I was frankly scared of this guy. Every inch of my body screamed at me that this man, for some unknown reason, wanted to hurt me. Of course, fear wasn't reason enough to change apartments, but on more than one occasion I sat down to seriously ponder the possibility of it.

One night in September, when the breeze started to blow cool, I got home after midnight. I had been out having a few beers with the boys. When I entered the building, I felt a chill and immediately remembered the stranger. And, I swear, nothing down there had reminded me of him. It was instinctive and inexplicable.

I closed the door behind me. Looking all around me, I climbed the stairs. When I entered the room, just as I was about to sigh in relief, I sensed something was off. I turned on the lights. The apartment was a mess. The furniture had been cut open with a sharp object, a razor perhaps. The few dishes I had lay broken on the floor. The lock had been forced.

Just then I remembered the money and ran to my room.

In anger, shock, helplessness and fear, I sat down on the floor and allowed myself to cry. All my savings had been taken. He'd taken everything I had.

*****

The robbery taught me a great lesson: I could not continue to live in the United States illegally. It was mandatory, and urgent, to get my papers. But to do that, I had to start over, from scratch, and focus entirely on that particular goal. Not having a legal immigration status, fear and ignorance prevented me from reporting the theft. And the owner of the building, though she meant well, did not help me at all: she didn't want me to report the incident, either. All of her tenants were undocumented. "*No, mijo, no sea bruto*, if the cops come, we all go to hell."

With no money and scared to stay in that place, I began to inquire among co-workers if anyone could rent me a room. Rambo (his real name) made an ill-humored comment I never forgot: "Well, Ricky, ask the guys who are single, guey."

I never knew if he said it because he had somehow found out about Onelia or if it was just a bad joke. The truth is, after that, I stopped asking.

A couple of weeks later, Víctor, a quiet and hardworking Ecuadorian, asked, "you still need a room, Ricardito?" "Well, yes, Víctor. I have to move," I replied. He nodded and told me he had a room for me. After three days, I was in his house and back on the arrimao list. He lived with his two children and his wife, Josefa.

Despite having to leave the comfort of my own little space, I was relieved. Before I moved, I was always worried at work, crestfallen: that son-of-a-bitch had taken all my savings. But at night, when I had to get back there, it was even worse: I hardly slept, afraid that he would break back in and leave me sleeping there forever.

At Víctor's house, as soon as I returned from work, I would hide in my room. It was as if the sensation of being a bother was stronger, more overwhelming, when I interacted with them. At least in the thick of solitude, I didn't have to think about it so much. I could entertain myself with my daydreams and my sorrows, with my what-ifs and my frustrations.

CHAPTER 22

THE IDIOT FORCED IT ON HIMSELF

Lieutenant Grant saw the snipers on the roof. He shook his head. He knew the situation had gotten out of control. With growing frustration, he stared at the reporters and their cameras. Even a chopper had arrived.

The crowd was growing, too, as if this were a sporting event or a concert.

Ever since the thief shot his weapon, tempers heated up. His men looked at him suspiciously. Rodney had even gone so far as to question him in front of the others. For that reason, with regret, he had given the order to enter.

The idiot forced this on himself. The robber's chances of survival had been drastically reduced. What Grant feared most was that the thief would kill a hostage. He didn't want that on his record or his conscience.

When he heard Sergeant Snyder say that they had the target on sight, for a fleeting moment he stopped to wonder if it was necessary, absolutely necessary, to kill him.

Although he didn't want to, he knew what the answer was. He knew the alternative was to risk the lives of the hostages.

"You got him on sight?" He asked rhetorically. "Jacob's got'im, Lieutenant".

Jacob was one of his best men. The sergeant, not so much. If the roles had been reversed, if it had been Snyder pointing the gun, saying he had the thief on his sight, maybe he would have said no.

"Take'im out!" Grant ordered; and just as soon, he sighed and swallowed hard… with regret.

Before a minute, the shot. And then exploding glass almost at the same time. People were alarmed. Someone yelled, someone cursed and then someone else cried in terror. Grant looked up at the third floor.
Before reacting, before asking if he had taken him out, Lieutenant Grant heard a voice screaming:

"Oh shit! Oh shit!"

CHAPTER 23

ALL'S GONE TO HELL

"They fucked me, manin," **were** the last words Monchi pronounced before spitting a mouthful of nasty dark blood and dropping dead.

Roberto spent an hour crying, sitting on the edge of the bed. Upset, frustrated, he yelled at the dead man, asked him why the hell he was leaving him alone.

After a while, he looked through his cousin's things and found the notebook where he knew Monchi kept everything jotted down. He searched until he found the name of Monchi's sister: Yrene. He thought about it for a few minutes before he called her. After the initial shock and cries, Yrene told him they'd be there as soon as possible.

After he hung up, it did not take him long to realize the situation he was in. He was in a house that had not been paid for in several months, where there were drugs and hidden weapons, and a man lying dead by way of a gunshot. He was an illegal alien, probably wanted for robbery by the police in New York.

"Shit," he said softly. Without wasting any more time, he got up, picked up a Puma bag his cousin used for the dirty clothes, threw in a few pieces of clothing, the cell phone charger, his passport, two pairs of tennis shoes, and a box of bullets. He tucked a gun in his waistband, counted his small savings—that he kept under the mattress—and divvied them between his battered wallet and his pockets.

He spent another precious fifteen minutes looking for any hidden money Monchi may have had but found nothing. He left then without looking back.

He arrived at the auto shop. Mr. Pelayo was in his office. His huge belly gave Roberto the impression there were several people in there with him. "What is it, Roberto?" The boss asked him. Roberto took a deep breath before speaking. Pelayo looked at him sideways, over his reading glasses.

"Boss, you think I could stay here for a couple of days?"

"Here?" Pelayo asked suspiciously. "Why here? You got in trouble with the police?"

Roberto felt his forehead start to sweat and his mouth go dry.

He said, "No, don Pelayo, no... things are not so good in the house with Monchi, and his family's coming… so, you know how it is..."

Tomás, one of the mechanics, came in abruptly, asked the boss for some references and left.

Pelayo seemed to meditate for a minute.

"I'm giving you a week, *muchacho*, but I can't give you no more than that. So, stay in one of the cars back there. But, listen, if the police come asking for you, I'm first to tell them where you are. I don't want no trouble. I know what Monchi was doing and that's how he got fucked up and look at him now. Hope he makes it. So… one week."

That night, Roberto lay on the reclined seat of a Mitsubishi pickup that had neither paint nor tires. The ceiling had been scrapped bare. It took him a little over an hour to fall asleep. When at last he did, he saw his father entering the house.

He was holding the machete...

*****

[Marcia was washing a truckload of clothes in the backyard. She whistled to the melody from the radio in the living room—Miriam Hernández sang, *el hombre que yo amo, sabe que lo amo. Me toma en sus brazos y lo olvido todo...*

The second coffee of the morning was already purring in the coffee maker. Augusto entered through the alleyway. He noticed Roberto's t-shirts and jeans hanging from the cords, how tall the weed had grown in the neighbor's patio, and even how much smaller the whole place seemed to him then.

He found her crouched, her back to him, squeezing a pair of shorts with her swollen hands. She didn't see him. Perhaps she didn't even see the shadow of the machete as it made its fatal arching journey to her neck.

After the blow, Augusto looked at her for a long time. His eyes focused on the distance that separated her severed head from her torso, barely two or three feet apart and a pool of blood that widened rapidly.

When the glistening blood was about to touch his shoes, he moved toward the alley.

What he didn't know, what hadn't happened before, was that Roberto was there this time. He had Monchi's gun in his hand. And then he fired the first shot...]

...Roberto woke up abruptly. He was sweating despite the cold. He had a lump in his throat and his eyes were teary. The gun was just another shadow between his thighs.

He noticed that the back of his neck ached and that the cell phone screen swore it was 6:43 a.m.

*****

At about one in the afternoon, don Pelayo sent him to the bank to look for deposit slips. He walked in and noticed two white women at the counter. A white burly man dressed as a security officer stood close to the entrance. Farther down, in a glass office, a regal white man in his sixties spoke into a very shiny phone. Roberto was the only Latino there. They all looked him up and down.

Wasting no time, the security guard approached him and asked him what he wanted. Maybe it wasn't like that, but it seemed to Roberto that the man's tone wasn't all that nice. Roberto told him about the deposit slips and, again, could have sworn the security guard looked at him askance and with distrust.

He motioned for him to stay where he was. Two more customers came in and looked at him like he was a circus animal.

Maybe it was at that precise moment Roberto decided to rob the bank. Maybe it was that feeling of not belonging in that place, the unwelcome feeling of discrimination from those people, that caused him to lose an iota of his judgement and make that decision.

The guard handed him the forms and waved him out. Roberto looked him in the eyes briefly, defiantly. The bear-like man stared back at him with the absolute conviction of superiority overflooding from his blue eyes. Then, without a word, Roberto left.

CHAPTER 24

TAKE ME TO SEE MY SON AGAIN

"No, no, noooooo!" The blonde screamed, hysterical, her hands on each side of her head. Roberto and Ricardo were in shock.

The brunette's body looked like that of a doll some careless little girl had thrown down on the floor and left behind to her fate. A mixture of brown hair, shiny-red blood, and brain-matter gleamed next to her almost preternaturally. The blonde was soaked in the poor dead girl's blood.

Quickly, Ricardo took off his shirt, tore it apart, and tied it tightly around Roberto's thigh.

"This is it, Roberto. We're done here. It's time for you to give yourself up. Let us go before they kill us all," he advised.

Roberto did not answer. He had laid the pistol on the floor by his right leg and now clutched his shot leg with both hands.

Ricardo knew he could take the gun now. But he had always been a man to play it safe, something told him Roberto would not last much longer.

"Go, viejo," Roberto told him. His voice distant. It was the exhausted voice of an old man.

At that moment, Ricardo saw him exactly for what he was: a poor young man whom hatred and society had driven to despair. For uncommonly long seconds, Ricardo saw that young man now old, even already dead in life. He knew that life had long conditioned him to this empty spot, that circumstances had overpowered him. He felt sorry for him. He felt sorry for the millions of Robertos and the millions of Ricardos wandering the streets of a city with life-sucking fangs, with ignorant people, with prejudiced people. He saw himself reflected in that boy, wondered what would have happened to him if his father had murdered his mother—what he would have done if life had raped him like that.

"Roberto, the police are coming up soon. Give me the gun and get down on the ground. It's the only way you can get out of this thing alive."

"Go, now, viejo, let me be. I'm done," he told him, his head facing the mirror-like floor.

Ricardo did not insist. He got up and, before walking at a brisk pace to where the blonde was, put his hand on Roberto's shoulder the way perhaps he would have done with a son of his own.

Crouching, he grabbed the blonde by the shoulders, who was still on her knees crying madly. Seeing the inert body of the brunette so close, he clutched his stomach.

"Come, come, let's get out of here. Keep your head down, please. Hurry!" He told her. She was gone. Her eyes were open but she saw nothing.

"Look at me, look at me, do you understand me? Do you understand me? Let's go!"

Ricardo desisted. It was evident that this woman could no longer reason. Then the lieutenant's voice rang out: "Let the hostages go! We will step back if you let'em go!"

Ricardo knew they were in as much danger as Roberto.

A few yards away, he saw a door leading to another set of stairs. He cupped the woman's chin in his hand and turned her face to him. The woman looked at him with horror.

"Come, follow me," he said.

Just as he was about to crouch-run alongside the blonde, he saw that Roberto had gotten up and was staggering towards them. He had the gun in his hand.

The woman hugged Ricardo—a young girl scared of the boogeyman.

"Take me with you, viejo. Please, take me; and maybe I'll get to see my little boy once more."

Incredulous, shocked, in horror, the blonde pulled away from Ricardo and threw herself on the floor, for she could see in Ricardo's eyes that he would help this man.

What do you know about pain and loneliness, woman? Ricardo thought, sadly, as he put his shoulder under Roberto's arm and helped him to walk.

They limped their way to the stairway. Before opening the door and disappearing through it, Ricardo took one last look at the woman. She was sobbing with her face between her knees.

The brunette had half the floor painted the brightest red Ricardo had ever seen.

CHAPTER 25

HOW'S THIS FOR A CHANGE, LIEUTENANT

"Oh, my fucking God! You what?" Snyder had just confirmed to him that Jacobs had shot a hostage.
"A fucking woman? Oh fuck, fuck, fuck!"

Grant couldn't believe this was happening. He did not want to believe such a thing could happen to him in a place like this. He reminisced on how he'd given up his unit, his friends, his entire detective career, everything, to come to this fucking place following some stupid sense of safety for himself and his family—because his wife had been squeezing his goddamn balls hard —had she not— to get away from the fucking violence and now look at him, right in the eye of some major fuck-up.

He looked everywhere. It was vital that this did not reach the news. At that very moment, as if purposefully summoned by the dark forces of hell, a woman in her early forties, with a coat so long that it sort of swept the ground, approached him.

"Hi, I'm Jessica Ryans for WNBB news. Care to let us in on what's going on, officer?"
"It's Lieutenant Grant, Ms. Ryans, and, as of right now, we are trying to resolve the situation as efficiently and smoothly as possible; so, if you'll excuse me."

Before the reporter could come back with some smart-ass response, the lieutenant moved away from her side.

He had told her the truth: they were trying to resolve the situation. He got to Snyder and told him that he was leaving him in charge, that he too would enter the building.

He gathered two more men and then all three of them walked briskly toward the back of the building.

CHAPTER 26

THE UNBEARABLE SILENCE

The owners of the produce business, Don Tico's brother, Pancho, and Don Tico's wife, Mrs. Beatriz, offered me to manage a new branch of *La marqueta* they were opening in a small town in Massachusetts, near Boston.

"You will be much better there, Ricardo, making more money and living in a quiet suburban area," they assured me. And they didn't lie.

The town was several hours away from the rush of the Big Apple. It was called Crownsville. It didn't take me too long to get used to the tranquility of that place—I even wondered if maybe I was just getting old.

I noticed the people there were more reserved but much friendlier over time. I loved the fact that I lived in a house. I left my latest tiny apartment (in a whole series of tiny apartments I'd moved in and out of throughout the years) to the spaciousness of a house with two rooms, a living room, a dining room, and a kitchen that looked like a baseball stadium. All around it, there were bushes, trees, grass, flowers of a hundred different shapes and colors, and, farther south, barely a nine-minute walk away, there was even a narrow and pretty brook with water so crysta-

lline I'd sit by its bank for hours on end just to observe such puri-
ty stream down, ceaselessly, endlessly.

The house also had a small patio and a canopy over an
old-style wooden porch. Now, that porch, that was my favorite
spot of all. It was there that, come nightfall, I'd sit on my rocking
chair, the one I'd bought back in the Bronx from some funny old
fellow—he told me it was very cheap because everything he sold
was stolen—and which I loved like a sister.

I would drink a beer or two every other night, listen to
boleros, watch the unmatched beauty of the starred cosmos and
think and rethink everything I'd done so far and all the things I'd
do from that moment on. That porch was the nest where most
of my daydreams took place, where my innermost fears were
battled or cowered from, and where, in absolute darkness (I
would at such times turn off the kerosene lamp I liked to use) I
allowed myself to cry again, once in a very blue moon.

This porch, the house, the whole place, for that matter,
often reminded me of the time I married Mariel's mother. I moved from my old neighborhood to what they called 'a residential
area', which is the same as to say: from the night life (*la bemberria*),
and the knife fights to five or six old men playing dominoes under tiny balconies where their wrinkling wives sat to contemplate
the street and make plans that their husbands would never agree
with.

I remembered in Crownsville that the same thing had
happened in both places, there and back then, during the first
few months of my move: I could not sleep.

My body and my mind were used to falling asleep in Villa
Consuelo, looking out the window at the drunkards and the who-
res, watching over rooftops for witches, thieves, and whining

cats, seeing the hustle and argument of crackheads and dealers, and listening to Aviles, Lavoe, La Lupe and Raphy Leavitt from the jukebox at that magical place they called "The Musical Secret"—the bar on the corner.

...no me escribas, yo prefiero no tener noticias tuyas, tengo miedo, mucho miedo, que tus cartas me hagan mal... in the womb of the dark early morning, Julita Ross sang with grave nostalgia and these words would come to me in the wind; and, falling asleep, I would dream of becoming someone in life.

Over time, I figured out what had kept me from sleeping in these places so distant and so different from one another: it was the silence.

The all-encompassing silence of tranquility did not let me sleep.

I hardly saw any *tígueres* or homeless in the corners of Crownsville nor was there the startling, steely noise of the trains. I still had to get up early, but *La marqueta* was close by as was practically everything else.

There were many whites and Hispanics—mostly Dominicans and Ecuadorians. Few blacks, Orientals, and Indians.

In the absence of buildings, the sky was of a clear light blue. And during the nights, that multitude of stars I mentioned before granted me great joy.

It's fair to say that in Crownsville I found relative peace and financial stability. I did not find happiness because, for the immigrant who cannot resolve their undocumented status, the concept contained in the word 'happiness' ceases to exist, and they live from solitude to solitude, interrupted by routines and sporadic bursts of joy.

Some of these sporadic joys came to me in the shape of several love affairs—if one can call those shaky, trade-like, exclusively-sexual matters "love affairs."

Yet, at the end of each night, my body and memory always went back to missing Onelia.

The real black mark was my inability to fix my immigration status. Before I went to Crownsville, a friend had warned me, "Bro, the problem with those little towns is that there is no one to do papers with."

He was right. And then again, he was not. My luck in the big city had not fared any better. In Crownsville, I met over a dozen women. None were willing to embark on that adventure. Some were already married and some were too scared of the potential consequences. I understood—I'd lived through too much in that respect in New York not to know how these things worked, how damn hard it all was, how downright scary.

I remember, to mention but one, this fine-looking woman by the name of Yasmin. Now this girl Yasmin was a cupcake of a woman: five feet tall, curvy shape, envy-provoking ass, the sweetest, most melodious of voices and attitudes, and the face of a corrupted cherub.

We met through one of my co-workers, Ronny, coolest guy in the *marqueta* at that moment. Yasmin and Ronny used to hang out together. They went dancing to a Boricua place they loved—they were both Puertoricans—and (she later told me), used to go chasing after potential boyfriends together. The afternoon we met, I saw Yasmin waiting outside by the mangos and asked her if I could assist her. She eyed me up and down and said she was fine, just waiting for her *amiga*. "Gloria?" I asked her, a bit confused because this girl, Gloria, the only woman there, only worked the morning shift. She seemed to study my face for a second and then, with a mischievous smile, said, "Ronny."

That smile, I later concluded, should have told me what to expect from Yasmin. She was a con artist, this girl. Ronny tried to warn me, I must say. He never straight up told me this girl was a problem, but he did hint that she was. He used to make comments like, "*no te enamores de las boricuas, viejo*" or "*la Yasmin nada más se quiere ella, nene.*" But they were friends. I'm sure he felt if he came out and told me to dump her, he was betraying her.

The thing is Yasmin and I hit it up pretty good. She was like fifteen years younger than me but still of an age that marrying her didn't seem like an outrageous, business-only transaction. In front of an immigration officer, we could have definitely passed.

In retrospect, I sort of knew deep down that Yasmin would betray me. I played her, too, I must say. I waited a full year to let her in on what I really wanted from her. So, we were really just playing one another: she wanted me to pay for her nails, take her dancing, and buy her nice clothes every now and then, and I wanted her to fuck and to eventually get my papers.

The day I gave her five thousand dollars was the they we went to the Bronx to get married. Ronny was our best man, and a friend of hers, Tania, her bridesmaid. Yasmin looked gorgeous in a short white dress and high heels. I looked like a corpse in a black suit and tie. As we walked up the fly of stairs, I could not take my eyes off her—and, foolishly, even lent myself to fantasizing that, maybe, just maybe, we could be together after all. And then, it happened: I heard someone shout Yasmin's name. We all looked back, alarmed. There was this dude, six feet tall, arms as thick as my thighs, holding a wooden bat on his left hand and cursing at the top of his lungs. Ronny said, "oh shit" and, as soon as I saw Yasmin run to the brute and get pushed violently into a navy Honda Accord, I knew I had lost my five grands.

At first, I asked Ronny everyday if she was Okay. A couple of weeks later, either out of pity or desperation, he looked me straight in the eyes and told me, "*Viejo, ya olvídate de esa mujer y de esos chelitos.*" That's when I knew I had been served. It had all been planned beforehand.

In Crownsville, out of the dozen women I dated, Rosa Betances was the only one who said yes. She lived five blocks from my house. I'd met her by chance at a gas station. She was having a very loud and public argument with her then sixteen-year-old daughter, Roxy, whom, at first glance, everyone knew was a public danger to any man.

I paid Rosa four thousand dollars on the wedding day, with the sweet promise of another six-grand right after my permanent resident card rested on the palm of my hand. Three weeks after the wedding, we submitted the paperwork for my change of status. It was the most hopeful I had ever been.

One night, drunk and crying over another fight with Roxy, Rosa came to knock on my door. After forty minutes of non-stop chatter and tears about how ingrate her daughter was and how unfair life could be, she wiped her eyes with the back of her hand and told me point blank that she was my wife, and then jumped on me. The beers I'd been drinking didn't help, either.

We spent four months like that: phonily married, acting like we barely talked to one another in public, and then fucking our brains out at night.

Then came the problem. La Rosa fell in love—madly in love—with a ridiculously handsome Armand Assante look-alike, who drove a beat-up Harley and wore a leather jacket even if it killed him.

The truth is this dude, Cole, who could have been fifty, sixty, or even a badly-fought forty, had a model stance and the airs of a Sicilian mobster. I wouldn't be surprised to learn he spent his nights in front of the mirror rehearsing gestures from the gangsters in Bugsy or Goodfellas.

The astonishingly naïve, good old Rosita told me that she would return my money because what we had could no longer be. Corleone there had proposed to her and, "Well, Ricardo," she explained, as melodramatic as they come, "this fine man is the love of my life."

The problem was that the love of her life rode her away in the chrome-and-black Harley before she could give me my money back, supposedly on vacation, and I never saw them again.

I had to spend another thousand bucks to divorce that deranged woman.

*****

I feel that of all the bad and sad things the decision to emigrate encompasses, uncertainty is the worst. Not only the uncertainty of whether or not you will achieve your dreams, or if you will at least stabilize yourself financially, but the other type of uncertainty: the constant fear of losing a loved one and experiencing the terrible helplessness of not being able to do anything about it, of not being able to go to them when they're terminally ill and give them that last embrace and say your final farewells, not being able to pay respects to your friends, not being there for those who wander in the paths of pain and loss.

This uncertainty teaches you the desolation of having to cry from a distance and swallow the bitterness of loneliness.

And yet, it wasn't only these things that made migration a complex and difficult experience. Hard, in the truest sense of the word.

Over time, I realized, too, that residing in New York had changed me as a human being. It had made me take notice, meditate, and eventually act upon things that in Santo Domingo I did not see, did not understand, or simply did not process.

For better or for worse, New York was a school. If there was a university of life, then this great city was the main campus of that university. It was there, for the first time, that the word racism, to mention just one among many things, took shape and meaning for me.

In the time that I lived in Santo Domingo, in the neighborhood, the concept of racism never had a place in my days. Not because it did not exist, but because I belonged to a specific lower social class, whose delimitations were so precise and hermetic that it was impossible to go any farther or further. I was poor. And what that meant was that everyone around me was poor, too. Furthermore, unlike New York, ninety-nine percent of the people around me were Dominicans like me. Black, light-skinned, indio, lavaíto, brown, moreno… whatever the denomination, whatever the color of our skins, we were still poor and still Dominicans.

So, growing up, and even as a grown-ass man, the idea of racism never even crossed my mind or the minds of the thousands of people in the barrios. It was known only as a concept of something that took place in other countries.

Of course, in retrospect, I know now that that's not entirely true. We may not have known what racism really was, but there were hints of it everywhere: in our everyday conversations and behavior, in our jokes and our social inner-structures. We said things back then that now are hard for me to articulate, even to remember; things like, '*el negro es comía de puerco*' (Black people are food for pigs) or *Negro aquí, los calderos* (The only black thing we want here are the cooking pots.) Now, even these, as harsh and insensitive as they are, were never used as agents of hate. They were things we thought funny—out of ignorance. Things we said to get a chuckle out of someone. And they did get chuckles, and the objects of these stupid jokes shrugged it off or said *tu maldita mai* or simply kept on doing whatever it was they were doing and that was that. If anyone ever felt bad about any of it, no one could ever tell. We all had more serious practical concerns in our everyday lives, serious lack… like food, shoes, education, and money.

Racism probably existed back in DR, who could really tell? The closest experience, the closest feeling of discrimination we knew, we only encountered when we felt the urge to go past the social boundaries the city and society imposed on us—we felt it, hot on our flesh, burning, as the "*jevitos*" and the "*hijitos de papi y mami*" glanced at us with unmasked disgust.

Sooner than later, we would experience the full force of that unspoken reality: being black and being poor walked hand in hand; and the jevitos, the children of the rich, even those of middle class, well, they wasted no time in making it obvious.

So, when one of us veered too far beyond those limits and brushed too closely against those who, subtly, in a condescending and even subconscious way, were indeed racists or classists, there were established mechanisms to let us know we were trespassing.

In a sense, I feel Santo Domingo was designed for the prejudiced to live far from those of us who were discriminable. In such a clear-cut society, in which the regulars didn't mix up with "royalty", you never really heard about these things.

As I said, in the neighborhood we were all the same. That was the big difference: there were no whites, there were no blacks. We were all only Dominican. There was no hate. Only hunger and inherited, unnamed prejudice.

No one I knew, as far as I can remember, ever consciously mistreated others because they were black. No one was actually hated for being black. I know they say any form of racism, to any degree, is still racism, and that may be true. But even those hardcore anti-racism advocates must admit there is a difference between making a joke and killing a person, between acting out of ignorance and acting out of hate.

What I do remember, and it's the closest thing to the sort of prejudice I came to learn and experience later in New York, is the very public and, of course, no less terrible, hatred toward Haitians.

Issues of identity, culture, religion, history, and preconceptions, but also ignorance and the influence of the governments of both nations and their self-interests, have ingrained this century-old hatred between us and our neighbors.

However, there is much more to that than a mere mention of racism. Because racism does not cover the amalgam of angles that conflate in that conundrum.

Racism, per se, I feel, was not found in the island the way I discovered it as soon as I set foot in New York. What I saw back there was not even remotely what was happening in the Big Apple.

Only after stepping on North American soil did I begin to think in those terms; did I begin to see people and distinguish them by the color of their skin—and even this, this distinction, is not racism, for it has nothing to do with hatred.

Only in a country where everyone spoke distinctively about other people by mentioning what race they belonged to or what color their skin was did I come to realize what the notion of racism really was. And I was shocked. I was shocked to find myself in such a short time going along with this, saying that the Indians smelled like curry and would con you out of your hard-earned money, or white people were only nice as long as things went as they expected, or, oh that's blacks, they're the only ones with their guard up, always looking for a fight.

I wondered—I recriminated myself—*am I being racist?* But I had no parameters then to know whether this was racism or not. The only thing I knew, for sure, was that I hated nobody because of their color. So, was it racist to say I disliked whites because they looked at me weird when I spoke my broken English? Or was I a racist if I expressed disgust over the way the hindu people smelled? Because no matter how long they spent in this country, their accents never got better? Was it racism to say I disliked blacks because they were aggressive, overtly demanding and prone to violence? I felt there was a general misconception about what 'being racist' actually meant and entailed. A misconception that has been poisoning the North American society for decades on end.

While working at the marketplace in the Bronx, I had to deal with all kinds of people. Little by little, I started noticing trends, attitudes, actions, even gestures and forms of speech that were repeated over and over, over and over again. Certain things, then, I realized, only certain people did. Perhaps they were not exclusive of only those people, but, in the recurrence of said things, mostly the same people were involved.

A university professor, last-named Aguirre, who used to buy oranges, mangoes, and tangerines on Thursday afternoons, and with whom I loved to speak, one day said to me, "Ricardo, don't blame yourself too harshly. If we follow societal conceptions, we are all racists in one way or the other, unwillingly and without thinking. We have been raised this way and it is difficult to separate ourselves from that upbringing. Also, not everything you see here, hermano, is racism. There are stereotypes, which are impressions that certain ethnic groups give us over and over again. Those things predispose us. As soon as someone sees a Dominican dude, they think he's loud and that he'll be late. When you see African Americans, you think they're violent. Of the Puerto Ricans, people say they're conceited or that they like to live off the government. About the whites, we say they are calculating, racists, and psychopaths.

We mistake these things for racism, and to some extent, they are somehow linked, but they are not the same. In time, one tends to include each individual one sees within the stereotype that one creates of that race or that ethnic group. It is inevitable to form these judgments because, unfortunately, they come from the interaction and repetition of behaviors. Yet not all people do the same; and when we point at someone because others have done this or that, we make the mistake of labeling them. That's probably where the problem lies."

*****

In 2009, my grandfather died. I don't remember having cried so much in my entire life. I don't remember ever feeling so helpless, so stupid, so miserable. Over and over again, I asked myself the same questions: "What in hell did you come to this damn country for? Looking for what? If dreams are everywhere, if all a man has is his family."

Abu had been everything to me and in the desire to chase after the ghost of money, I missed out on the last decades of his life.

Not so long ago, he had asked my mother to call me. That was a miracle because that man hated telephones. That day, he asked me if I was doing well, if I'd met a good woman. He asked me to please take care of myself, and told me he was happy because I was where I wanted to be. I knew then that was his way of saying that he missed me. I wonder now if he was also saying good-bye.

*****

Sitting in the restaurant of Peruvian food I frequented, one afternoon, I saw El Corbejú. I was surprised to find him so far from New York.

It had been at least twenty years since that meeting in Villa Consuelo. The truth is he wasn't the same man. He was just a lousy-made clone of who he had been.

177

"I know you, right?" When I smiled at him, he recognized me. Maybe I gave him the same sad smile I had given him twenty years earlier. "Shit, boy, you are Ricardo, the son of *el viejo*."

He asked about everyone in the neighborhood. When I told him Abu had passed, he was genuinely sad. "That viejo, shit, he was the best thing in that neighborhood, mijo."

We talked for a while until finally he stood up, fixed his coat, and said, "Shit, time flies, eh. I remember you told me you wanted to come to Nuevayol, and look. It's not the same as it was before, man." He put his right hand on my shoulder and took his first step out. I smiled at the understanding that, to this day, most of us Dominicans thought of the entire USA only as Nueva York.

I saw that he was limping; his walk slow and weary, like someone who carries a backpack full of rocks on his shoulders. It seemed to me that, instead of two or three years, he was at least twenty years older than me.

He was already at the door when I said, "At least, I didn't die blind." And then I offered him a respectful smile.

He looked back, nodded in agreement, and smiled back, bitterly. Three of his front teeth were missing.

*****

A few days ago, talking to my mother on a video call, she said, "Mijo, stop mortifying yourself. If God wants you to come back here, He will show you the way. Just pray and take it easy. At least now with this technology, you can see me and Mariel

178

more often. *Esa muchacha*, gee, she's a grown woman already...
and so smart."

*****

That same night, in bed, I took notice of a fact that
should have been fully engraved in my mind, yet wasn't: almost
twenty-four years had passed since I left Santo Domingo in
search of the American dream. Twenty-four years without hugging my mother or my daughter. Twenty-four years of calling a
handful of good people my best friends without ever having
another beer with them or shaking their hands. Twenty-four
years since I bribed an American consul and said good-bye to *my
abuelo*, not knowing that I would never see him again.

Interestingly, I thought that a few years before, over a
realization like this, I would have cried. The truth was that I no
longer felt like crying.

I thought that in life everything is a matter of endurance
and adaptation: one gets used to, puts up with, or withstands any
situation when one thinks there are no more choices.

In all those years, I learned the value of solitude—learned through many an ordeal how incredibly resilient we human
beings are. I learned so much from people: our prejudices, our
phobias, our bad and good habits... I learned that love is both a
lottery and a leap of faith—that it is easier to flee from it than
confront it. But fleeing hardly ever has a happy ending.

I had concluded at this point, or rather accepted, that
leaving my homeland had been a mistake, a gross mistake—
whose price was too costly. I had missed the most important

179

milestones in my daughter's life. I was not there for the death of my grandfather. I had missed thousands of afternoons of talking with my mother, sharing coffee, crossword puzzles, and her food. I had lost the life I could have had with my friends, the nights at the *cerita*, the quiet presence of the neighborhood when the hours were still early and we, kids, chased after one another, chests and feet bare, our stomachs empty, our eyes gleaming with sheer, contradictory happiness.

I had lost everything for nothing. I had lost it all over the pursuit of a dream that a damn drug dealer with a few gold chains and colored shoes sold me over two decades before.

That night I did not cry. I realized that I had, indeed, lost it all... even my tears.

The next day, Mariel called me. When I saw her name on the cell phone screen, I felt my chest go cold. I replied with the same scared urgency I always did, "Hello, mi amor, everything okay?" Mariel laughed and said, "*Papi, pero, ¿qué es?* Every time I call you, you pick up the cell phone like someone's getting killed." "Ay mija! Yes, I'm sorry. What's up? What are you up to?"

She was calling to remind me about the wedding. I could hear it in her voice, the hope that I would surprise her, that I would tell her I was coming or, even better, that I would just show up. My beautiful daughter was getting married. It was a bittersweet feeling, just like everything else. She had introduced the groom to me over Facetime—a not-so-handsome young man by the name of Cristian with a degree in engineering and a million-dollar smile. He was two years older than Mariel and was head of a department in a big marketing company. They seemed madly in love and wanted to join their destinies for good. Well, the eternal bond would take place the following Saturday. I had asked her to remind me (my memory, she knew, was utterly unreliable) because I wished to send them a monetary wedding gift. She had tried to convince me that it was not necessary, but, come on, what else but money could I offer them if I could not be there with them? Around 5:25 P.M., I told the guys at work I was going to the bank before they closed. I had to withdraw some money and send it to Mariel. When I arrived, only a young woman was ahead of me in the waiting line. Another lady was stepping out.

I found it odd that there was only one cashier. At the door, the security guard seemed concerned about the weather for he kept looking out at the sky.

After a while, a Hispanic-looking guy came in, somewhat suspiciously. I was on my cell phone looking at photos of Mariel on Social Media. *She's a woman now. It'd be nice to see her in her wedding gown, walk her to the altar.* That's what I was thinking when the guy pulled out a gun, put it on the back of the security guard's neck, and yelled that this was a robbery. I put the cell phone away and shook my head. The guy disarmed the security guard and yelled at the cashier to collect the money for him. "Give me all the fucking money, bitch."

A mixture of embarrassment and anger crept up onto my chest. The boy was Dominican. His accent betrayed him. I could tell. Somehow, perhaps unfairly, I thought it almost wickedly funny that two very different Dominicans had converged in this place.

CHAPTER 27

TWO SIDES OF THE SAME COIN

Lieutenant Grant arrived at the back of the building with the two agents and saw Roberto and Ricardo as they descended the emergency stairs of the smaller, adjacent building.

It crossed his mind that this advantage angle had made it possible for him to see them; and wondered if such an idiotic attempt at escaping may have actually worked—had he not lost his temper and come all the way out here, these two might have, in fact, run away.

Ricardo raised both arms automatically and begged for Roberto to drop the gun as soon as he realized the lieutenant had spotted them.

The blood from Roberto's thighs trickled down the metal steps.

Lieutenant Grant and the two officers ran towards the building, drawing the attention of the rest of the snipers (they could not believe they had missed the two men), then they stopped. Grant started to go up only to pause briefly. He was twenty steps bellow them. Slowly, he resumed his way up, yelling for the two of them to drop their weapons.

Ricardo yelled back, "I'm not armed, I'm not armed... not armed!"

Roberto felt dizzy. He wanted to scream. He wanted to surrender, too, but the thought of prison kept the gun in his hand. At that moment, as he saw Ricardo's teary, scared eyes, he felt an unlikely desire to ask for forgiveness. He wanted to say to this old man, this good old man, that he was sorry. And as their gazes locked, he thought that maybe Ricardo was able to see it in his eyes, too: the fear, the regret.

Instead, Roberto looked at the sky looming blue and endless over Crownsville. For an instant that seemed eternal, he saw once again the smiles of his mother, Daniel, and his beloved Ruth. Shanikwa's sexy smile was there, too; and, for the first time, he only recalled the way he felt about her, not the bad stuff, but the sweet, lasting feelings.

When he finally looked down at Lieutenant Grant, he did not know how, but God had given him the chance of his life. It wasn't the lieutenant at all, but Augusto. It was his father at the bottom of the stairs. He was waving the blood-stained machete at him.

Roberto smiled and fired at the same time.

Ricardo shook his head so many times, as he tried to escape, but there was nowhere to run.

In the involuntary expectation of death, as an array of gunshots resounded like timeless fireworks, Ricardo, too, was granted that final magical moment in which reality was usurped by love: he saw Abu and Mariel holding hands. He saw Dulce in her little kitchen, making coffee and telling him he was never *arrimao* in her house; he saw his *tía* Carla tapping his shoulder and heard her calm voice saying: "it will all be fine in the end." And then he saw Onelia, his mute love, *flaca* and sexy and lonely as hell, his one and only true love, sitting at her window, living life the way perhaps a flower vase or a coffee maker would.

And then the lieutenant, in desperate disbelief, saw his wife and daughter, mysteriously, in the same blue sky, as he went free-falling towards the ground.

Then, finally, the shooting stopped. There was not a single sound in the entire world. Good old Lieutenant Grant lay in a grotesque position on the pavement. He had died with his eyes open and a word stuck between his lips.

Roberto and Ricardo lay dead, too, on the iron stairs. Side by side. Their eyes open wide, fixed perhaps on something not of this existence.

Whoever knew them, whoever saw them like that, would have thought that they were the two sides of a coin… holding on to a myth.

The End.

This book was concluded in 2024 and its edition was under
the care and attention of Books&Smith.

For promotional or publishing information, please, e-mail us at:
booksandsmith@hotmail.com.

www.booksandsmith.com

www.ingramcontent.com/pod-product-compliance
Lightning Source LLC
Chambersburg PA
CBHW031156010826
48971CB00012B/737